Capri Nights

By

Cara Marsi

Published by The Painted Lady Press
United States of America

Print ISBN: 978-0-9915975-7-4

This book is a work of fiction and all characters exist solely in the author's imagination. Any resemblance to persons, living or dead, is purely coincidental. Any references to places, events or locales are used in a fictitious manner.

Edited by Judi Fennell
Cover by Harris Channing
Formatted by Aileen Fish

A San Francisco sous chef discovers she might have bitten off more than she can chew when a yummy Italian man stirs up a recipe for romance on the delicious Isle of Capri.

Sous chef Cat Connors has spent a lifetime feeling like a stale cracker on a plate of fancy hors d'oeuvres among her stepfamily. But when she travels from San Francisco to the sunny Isle of Capri, she's determined to finally shed her dowdy image and spice up her life. She has big plans for her future as a chef. Those plans don't include a yummy Italian with a mouth-watering body and a smile that melts her insides like gelato under the hot Capri sun.

When Alex Viteli retreats to his villa on Capri to escape the notoriety and legal troubles brought on by his family, the last thing he needs is a beautiful, tempting dish of a woman. Alex may be the scion of a wealthy Italian family, but that won't matter if he can't cook up a scheme to clear his father's name and keep himself out of prison.

Though they fit together like strawberries and chocolate, Cat and Alex may not have time for more than a quick bite of romance. Cat's future is in San Francisco. Alex can't leave Italy. But the sultry Capri nights might tempt them both to savor just one more sweet taste of love.

CHAPTER ONE

Isle of Capri, Italy

"Mi scusi, signorina! Signorina, scusi!"

The urgent male voice broke into Cat Connors' thoughts and rose above the babel of languages from the tourists crowding Capri's main square, *La Piazetta*. The man's voice got closer. Her knowledge of Italian was limited, but it sounded like he wanted a woman's attention. He couldn't be talking to her. She kept walking.

Someone touched her arm, stopping her.

With a gasp, she turned around. Her gaze collided with a black T-shirt stretched over a hard, muscled chest. Slowly, she raised her eyes to take in six feet of male hotness. He stared down at her with the hazel eyes of a Roman god. He must have descended from the heavens, with those chiseled cheekbones, wavy dark blond hair and full lips that promised heavenly delights. He epitomized the kind of gorgeous guy she'd expect to find on this romantic island.

He held out a phone to her. *"Ha perso il suo*

telefono?"

She felt in her pants pocket. Empty.

"My phone! Thank you. Where did you find it?" Hoping he spoke English, she took the phone from him.

"It fell out of your pocket." Speaking perfect English, his deep voice with a hint of lilting accent sent a jolt of pleasure coursing through her.

Clutching the phone, she patted her pocket again. The movement of her hips as she walked must have pushed the phone out. She should have known to secure it better. Her eyes met Mr. Roman God's. "Thank you again."

His killer grin made her insides melt like gelato in the hot Italian sun.

He shrugged in that offhand way Italians had perfected. "No problem. You are American?"

"I am."

Someone shoved against her and she almost lost her balance. Mr. Roman God cupped her elbow, steadying her.

"It's not every day I have the pleasure of meeting a beautiful American," he said.

Her beautiful? No one except her mother had ever called her that. "Uh—thank you," she stammered.

"I would like to buy you a glass of wine." He studied her with those incredible hazel eyes fringed by thick dark lashes.

This smokin' guy was picking her up in the middle of Capri's main square? Men rarely hit on studious, quiet Cat Connors. Must be something in the water here.

Anxiety fueled by shyness compelled Cat to say

no. If she was ever to become the new Cat, she had to forge ahead and take chances. Forced to come here on this family trip, she'd decided it would be the catalyst she needed to complete her metamorphosis into a new Cat. She'd finally pull free from the shadows of her glamorous stepsisters and be her own person—a woman who no longer tried to please others but lived her own life. A little harmless flirtation with Mr. Roman God would be the perfect place to start. In this square packed with tourists, she'd be safe. She had time before she had to meet Angelina.

"Okay, I'd like to have a drink with you."

They sat at an outdoor table in a nearby café that fronted the square. Mr. Roman God said something in rapid Italian to the waiter who brought over a bottle of chilled pinot grigio, opened it, and presented the cork to her companion, who sniffed the cork and nodded that the wine was acceptable. The waiter filled two glasses and shoved the opened bottle into an ice-filled bucket on a stand next to them.

When he left, Mr. Hotness leaned his elbow on the table and raised his glass. "My day has become more interesting."

She touched her glass with his. "To interesting days."

He chuckled and sipped his wine. "My name is Alessandro," he said, setting his glass onto the white tablecloth. "My American friends call me Alex."

"Nice to meet you, Alex," she said, sounding very proper and feeling anything *but*. "I'm Caitlyn. Everyone calls me Cat."

She held out her hand. Instead of shaking it, he

raised it to his lips. When he planted a gentle kiss on the back of her hand, his touch sent electricity rocketing up her arm. She pulled free before they spontaneously combusted in front of the hordes of tourists crowding the square. Damn, his touch was explosive.

She took a big swallow of wine, as if the liquid could quench her sudden thirst for something wild and forbidden that flowed through her veins with the force of a storm off the Gulf of Naples.

"Cat." He said her name as if it were a scrumptious treat he savored. "The name suits you." He grabbed the wine bottle and refilled her glass. "Are you enjoying our beautiful island?"

"What's not to enjoy? It's paradise."

He laughed softly.

His easy charm was the ingredient she needed to bolster her confidence. She tilted her head and ran a hand down her thick braid that fell over her shoulder. Interest flared in his eyes. She could lose all her inhibitions in those eyes.

A seductive grin played around his mouth and he lifted his glass in salute. "To your beautiful red hair."

"It's not really red. More of a chestnut brown." Heat started at her neck and spread over her face. *Way to go, Cat. Real sophisticated.* She'd never learned to accept compliments. But then she'd had very few considering most people compared her to her stylish stepmother and stepsisters and found her wanting. No more. The new Cat would appreciate compliments, thank you very much, and show those stepsisters she could play on their rarified turf.

He looked down at her left hand, bare of any rings.

"You are alone?"

Smokin' or not, he was a stranger. She'd be careful. "My family is here too, for my stepsister's wedding."

"Family and weddings. They are very important in Italy too. You are not married?"

"No, I'm not." Considering her fiancé dumped her almost at the altar, she wanted nothing to do with marriage. But she wouldn't tell Alex any of that. "I'm a chef," she said instead. "I'm concentrating on my career now. Marriage will have to wait."

"A chef. *Molto bene.* Very good."

"Thanks." Cooking had always been her passion, and she knew she was good. She had no problems accepting compliments on her cooking.

"Where in the States do you live?" he asked.

"San Francisco."

"I've been there several times on business. A beautiful city, but not as beautiful as Capri."

She laughed. "You'd better not let anyone from San Francisco hear that."

He pushed aside his glass and leaned closer. "I would like to show you around my island, then you will see how beautiful it is."

She ran a finger around the rim of her glass. "Thank you for the invitation, but I don't really know you."

"I understand. Have dinner with me here tomorrow night? Then we can get to know each other."

His eyes, his mouth, his charm tempted. "I'm not sure," she said.

"I'll put my number into your phone. It will be your choice to call me."

Like ingredients thrown into a stewpot, her mind

jumbled. She wanted to see him again. He could be a gigolo preying on female tourists. *Take a chance, Cat,* a small voice inside her said. As she started to slide her phone to him, it dinged, signaling a text. When she read the text, she gasped and retrieved her purse from under the table.

Holding onto her phone and purse, she stood. "I have to leave, Alex. I'm meeting a friend. She's taking me shopping. I'm late. She texted to say she's waiting for me and her car is blocking traffic. Thanks for returning my phone and for the wine." She was babbling.

Feeling oddly like Cinderella running from the ball, Cat hurried away, winding between the tables.

"Cat, wait!" Alex shouted.

She'd already joined the throngs on *La Piazetta.* She started to glance back to Alex but didn't give in to the temptation. He'd provided a brief, pleasant distraction. She'd be here for a short time. She'd never see him again. That was okay. *Liar.*

*****

Alex sank back onto his chair. He didn't know the beautiful American's last name or where she was staying. At one time, he would have gotten her full name and phone number right away. That was in the days when his life was simple. It wasn't so simple any more.

He studied the wine in his glass as if he could read his fortune there. Maybe his luck was changing. Fate had brought Cat to him. Maybe it would bring her back. Her features—bright, animated, without guile—were a balm to his soul. Half his family and most of his friends had abandoned him. He needed a woman like Cat in his life.

He'd spotted her, walking with a bouncy step, as he'd stood by one of the outdoor cafes, his thoughts on his uncertain future. With her fresh-faced innocence, sweet like the flowers that grew in abundance along the square, she stood out among the boisterous, overdressed crowds. Something in him had responded to the wonder on her face as she took in the sights around her. Fate had intervened and plopped her phone down almost in front of him.

Cat radiated a quiet beauty with her high cheekbones and large blue eyes. She didn't seem to recognize her own allure, unlike so many of the women he knew, who used their beauty to get what they wanted, women who wanted his money and all it would bring them. Like his fiancée, who'd fled when his troubles started.

In less than a week, he'd know his fate. Prison or freedom? No matter what the authorities decided, Alex's life had changed forever. He'd done the right thing. He had to clear his father's good name. His father was no longer here to defend himself. It was up to Alex to restore his family's reputation and the reputation of their company. It was what his sainted mother would have wanted. If only his extended family believed in him.

CHAPTER TWO

Wearing the pale green sundress that hugged her body, and the sky-high gold sandals that made her legs look longer, Cat felt like a fairy-tale princess for the first time in her life. She twirled in front of the mirror in her bedroom at the villa her father and stepmother had rented.

During their shopping excursion earlier today, Angelina had laughingly called herself Cat's fairy godmother. Thanks to Angelina's help as they shopped in the upscale boutiques of Capri, the old Cat, the young woman who hid behind unflattering clothes and hair, had disappeared. Believing the only way she could gain her father's attention and love was to be a serious person who studied hard and got good grades, Cat had deliberately eschewed fashion and focused on her studies. Unwilling to compete with her sophisticated, socialite stepsisters, Cat became the opposite of them.

She'd done well in college, then attended law school at her father's insistence, and started working at the family firm, but all her hard work hadn't earned his love or acceptance. Cat wondered if she reminded her father too much of her mother, the woman whose heart he'd broken by his infidelity.

When she'd confessed to Ethan, her ex-fiancé, that she'd rather attend culinary school than practice law, he insisted she go along with her father's plans for her. Ethan said with her law degree and his medical degree, they'd be able to afford the lifestyle they wanted. Or rather, he wanted. Then he found someone else and dumped her.

Cat narrowed her eyes at her reflection. *Sheesh.* She was almost thirty and she'd had it with doing what others wanted. Leaving law for culinary school was her first step to independence. This island with its sunshine, flowers, and hot men, plus her new wardrobe, further peeled away her layers to expose the real Cat, the woman she'd always wanted to be.

With a small laugh, she smoothed her hand over her newly cut and styled hair. Her waist-length hair had been trimmed to just below her shoulders. Very straight with light feathering framing her face, the shorter cut made her eyes seem bigger and bluer. The red highlights the stylist put in enhanced her hair's natural color.

Alex had complimented her on her hair. Warmth flowed through her as she remembered his sexy smile and that deep voice. She had a vision of running off with him for adventure. Sure beat having to make nice at the party tonight with her stepmother's snooty friends.

Wanting a few more minutes of calm before heading into the den of vipers that was her stepfamily, Cat stepped outside to the tiny patio off her room. She leaned on the ornate white iron railing and inhaled the tart scent of lemons from the trees in the gardens below.

Just as the unflattering clothes and hair had been her disguise, her new clothes and hair style were now her armor against the barbs from her stepfamily.

She should have given Alex her number, but maybe it was best she hadn't. His overt sensuality and her reaction to it scared the crap out of her. Damn it, she'd never be the new Cat if she didn't overcome her fears.

With a heavy sigh, she headed downstairs to where the family had gathered prior to the party.

Nolan Connors, her stepmother, lived a lavish lifestyle that most people knew only from reality shows. Appearance and social standing meant everything to Nolan. By putting on this elaborate and very expensive wedding for the older of her two daughters, she'd insured she and her daughters would get photo spreads in *Vogue, W,* and *People.*

Cat couldn't care less about money or getting her name in the gossip columns. She wanted to build her career and eventually open her own restaurant. And maybe someday get married, but marriage was on the back burner for now.

As Cat strolled through the living and dining rooms to the lattice-covered patio, the cloying scent of roses assailed her. Nolan, always over-the-top, had had roses cut from the bushes in the extensive gardens and set into vases throughout the first floor. Sneezing, Cat stepped outside.

Beyond the mosaic-floored patio, the water of the Olympic-size pool sparkled gold in the setting sun. Statues of Ancient Roman gods and goddesses were set around the pool, arrogant figures from a bygone era looking down on the modern men and women and finding them wanting. Servants bustled around the tables that rimmed the pool. Cat knew the guest list tonight was small and that some of the guests were European royalty.

"Cat, darling, what have you done with your hair?"

Her stepmother, fifty-something leader of San Francisco society, her long blonde hair curling softly around her expertly made-up face, glided toward Cat clutching a crystal martini glass. Nolan's slim white silk gown with a thigh-high slit exposed one of her shapely legs. A tall woman, the white stiletto sandals she wore made her height over six feet. Large sapphire chandelier earrings dangled from her ears. Cat figured one of those earrings would pay the rent at her small San Francisco apartment for six months. At least the apartment was all hers. She'd pay her own way now with no help from her father. Not that he'd been much help when she was growing up. Money had been tight at times for Cat and her mother.

Nolan gave Cat air kisses, then retreated back to the glass-block bar in the corner.

"Nice dress, Cat," Tinsley, Nolan's daughter, and the bride-to-be, said with a smirk. A princess surveying her domain, Tinsley, her streaked blonde hair pulled into a high pony tail, and wearing a red dress that barely covered her assets, lounged on one of the chintz-covered chaises. "Where'd you get the clothes? Did Angelina lend them to you?"

Cat lifted one shoulder in a shrug. "They're my clothes." She took a glass of champagne from the tray held by Paolo, the butler.

Bailey, Nolan's other daughter, joined them and accepted a flute of champagne from Paolo. With a haughty toss of her head, she strolled to Cat. "Decent clothes for a change. At least you'll be presentable tonight with all the important people coming."

Cat rolled her eyes. "Seriously, Bailey? You're going to go there? Let's call a truce for one night."

"Whatever. I can't wait to meet the prince Mother invited for me."

Cat almost choked on the champagne she'd sipped. "Prince? For you?"

"*Prince* Sandro Viteli. From the Italian royal family."

"Italy no longer has a royal family," Cat said.

"If they still had one, Prince Sandro would be part of it."

"I hear he's smokin' too," Tinsley said, walking up to them.

Cat swallowed the rest of her drink and took another glass from Paolo. She needed all the liquid fortifications she could get to deal with this crowd. A prince, for God's sake. There'd be no stopping Nolan if one of her daughters snagged a royal.

Bailey settled onto one of the stools at the bar. "When do you start your new job as cook, Cat?"

With a sigh, Cat said, "You know I'm a sous chef at Vault, one of San Francisco's finest restaurants."

Nolan gave a dismissive wave of her hand. "I've gotten bored with Vault. It's so last year."

Fighting for patience, Cat drew a careful breath. "The new head chef there is Bobbie St. James." She named one of the world's most famous chefs. "I had to compete against a lot of talented people for my job. I guarantee you won't be bored again at Vault."

"Maybe your father and I will have dinner there sometime after we get back home."

As if on cue, Cat's father, along with Tinsley's fiancé, Huntley Mortimer, *the fifth*, walked onto the patio. They each held a large glass of what looked like whiskey. Cat could see her father was already drunk. From Huntley's glassy eyes and the way he rubbed his nose, she figured he'd been snorting his drug of choice, cocaine.

The smarmy expression on Huntley's face as he studied Cat made her want to take a shower. He'd been coming onto her for the past year, since he and Tinsley had gotten engaged. "Looking sexy tonight, Cat," he said. "What happened to the schoolmarm braid?"

"It's cut. Okay?" Anxious to escape the barracudas surrounding her, Cat walked down to the pool. The statues reflected in the calm water, silent sentinels. *You only have to get through these next few days, then you can go home and be done with these people,* they seemed to say.

An hour later, the party was in full swing. Cat tried to be as gracious to the guests as her mother had taught her. Molly Connors, an artist in Sausalito, California, entertained often. Dealing with this self-absorbed crowd, Cat missed her mother. Molly had a ready smile for everyone and didn't take herself too seriously. Cat, sitting at a small table, shifted in her seat to get a better view of her dad. He stood unsteadily talking to two men whose names she couldn't remember. She wondered for the hundredth time what sort of man her father would be if his infidelity hadn't destroyed their little family.

Movement by the doorway caught her attention. Cat dropped the small crab cake she'd been about to put into her mouth. The flush of adrenaline that flowed through her propelled her from her chair. Alex, dressed in beautifully tailored tan pants and wearing a black shirt opened at the neck, stood in the doorway. Nolan clutched his arm and grinned like a wolf who'd just scored a meal. Bailey, on his other side, shook her head to let her platinum blonde hair fall seductively around her face, a movement she'd perfected.

"Everyone!" Nolan said. When the guests quieted, Nolan pulled Alex forward. "*Prince* Alessandro Viteli, our honored guest, is here."

Honored guest? *Prince* Alessandro Viteli. The *Prince Sandro* Nolan had invited for Bailey? Alex sure wasn't the gigolo Cat had feared.

Alex nodded to the group, every bit the royal. "Please call me Alex," he said to Nolan. With a flourish, he presented her with a bottle of wine.

"Gotham Project Gazerra," Nolan breathed. She grabbed the bottle and held it at arm's length, staring at it as if it were a gold bar crusted with diamonds. Cat waited for her to swoon.

With Bailey clinging to his arm, Alex spotted Cat. He said something to Nolan and Bailey and extricated himself. Bailey's enhanced lips formed a pout and she stamped her foot.

"Cat!" Alex said when he reached her. "I have found you again." He took her hand and raised it to his lips for a soft kiss.

Cat thought *she* might swoon. "I'm glad to see you again. Bailey said *Sandro* Viteli was coming. I didn't know that was you."

Alex grabbed a glass of champagne from a passing waiter and cupped Cat's elbow, drawing her to the side. Cat slid a glance toward Nolan and Bailey. If looks could kill, she'd be at the bottom of the pool now.

"My family and my Italian friends call me Sandro, but no one calls me prince," he said. "My royal blood has no meaning now. I care nothing about that."

"I'm very surprised to see you here," she said. "How do you know my father and stepmother?"

"Davison Connors is your father?"

When she nodded, he said, "I've done business with your father's firm in the past. When he and his wife invited me to this party, I accepted, in the interest of maintaining a good working relationship." Alex's eyes sparked green-gold fire as he scanned Cat. "But you and I will not talk business. You are *bella*. Beautiful." He touched her hair, letting strands of it slip through his fingers. "You cut your hair."

"You don't like it?"

"I like it. I like everything about you. You are *molto bella* no matter your clothes or hair." He tapped his chest. "Your beauty comes from inside."

Her face heated. "Thank you." She really needed to learn to accept compliments.

"It is I who should thank you."

"Me? Why?"

"For being a friendly face in this sea of sharks. *Mi scusi*, Cat. I do not mean your family. I know most of the guests, and they are the sharks."

Cat laughed. "Don't be too sure about my family."

"Nolan Connors is your stepmother?"

"Yes. Bailey and her other daughter Tinsley are my stepsisters. Tinsley is the one getting married."

Alex touched her arm. "Excuse me while I say hello to your father and a few of the others. When I'm done, let's leave here. I want to show you the *real* Capri."

His hazel eyes gleamed with awareness in the soft light from the lanterns strung in the trees. An answering awareness gripped Cat. Leave this crowd and go off with Alex? "Okay."

A half hour later, Alex had made the rounds talking to the other guests, Bailey stuck to his side like peanut butter on bread. Cat wasn't worried. Alex had asked her and not Bailey to go with him. Cat noticed that while some of the guests seemed cordial to Alex, others ignored him.

Finally, free of Bailey, he strolled over to Cat where she stood trying to make small talk with an Italian journalist and his wife. When the couple saw Alex heading toward them, they stiffened and walked away.

The clench of Alex's jaw was the only sign he'd noticed the snub.

"Ready to leave?" he asked Cat.

"More than ready. Let me get my purse."

"I'll wait for you out front in the car."

Alex strode briskly away and Cat headed to her room. With her foot on the bottom step leading to the second floor, someone yanked on her arm, stopping her. Cat whirled to face Bailey. The fury flashing from the other woman's eyes could light a room.

"What do you think you're doing?" Bailey hissed.

"What are you talking about?"

"The prince belongs to me. He said you and he are leaving together." Bailey jabbed a finger into Cat's chest. "You tell him you're not going anywhere with him."

Flaring her nostrils, Cat grabbed Bailey's finger and pushed it away. "Chill out, Bailey. You don't tell me what to do."

A rush of giddy joy that she'd finally talked back to Bailey threatened to lift Cat off the ground. Damn, she should have told Bailey off a long time ago.

With a spring to her steps, Cat raced up the stairs, leaving a red-faced Bailey behind.

A few minutes later, purse in hand, she got to the front door when she heard footsteps behind her.

"Caitlyn! I want to talk to you," her father said.

Sheesh. She'd never get out of this place.

"What?" She faced him.

"Where do you think you're going?"

"Out with Alex."

"No, you're not."

"Excuse me."

"He's not for you."

She put her hand on her hip. "For God's sake, you're going to tell me he's *reserved* for Bailey?"

"I don't want him with Bailey either. Viteli is a possible felon, facing prison. I don't want you mixed up with him."

Prison? So not what she expected to hear. "Dad, if he's a possible felon, why did you and Nolan invite him tonight? And why does she want to fix him up with

Bailey?"

"Your stepmother invited him. She's enthralled by Viteli's heritage. If she can marry her daughter off to someone with royal blood, she doesn't care if he's the devil himself."

Cat stared into her father's blue eyes. "Cynical much? I don't know what Alex has done, but he sure doesn't act like a felon. Goodnight."

As she hurried into the humid night, doubts stirred an anxious mix in her. Alex couldn't be a criminal.

CHAPTER THREE

The engine running, Alex drummed his fingers on the steering wheel of his Ferrari as he waited for Cat. She came out of the house, walking with the sensuous grace he found so appealing, a sleek feline he'd like to make purr.

The heavy mantle of sadness that had covered him the past months lifted a little when he was with Cat. He wanted to absorb her innocence, and he wanted to know her, all of her—her thoughts, her likes, her dreams. He wanted to go back to a time when he trusted others. And when others trusted him.

Cat opened the car door and slid inside. "Let's go."

Her bright smile infused him with a sense of well-being he hadn't felt in a long time.

The sleek Ferrari easily negotiated the narrow roads and hairpin turns. Driving the winding roads of Capri had always relaxed him, until recently. With Cat beside him, some of his stress dissolved into the starry night.

She threw back her head to stare at the sky, exposed by the open top of the car. "My God, even the sky is more beautiful here than anywhere else. I've never seen so many stars, like diamonds strung across black velvet."

She sat straighter as the three rocks that formed *Faraglioni* came into view. They thrust through the water, sentries that had guarded Capri since the dawn of time. "Amazing," she breathed. "I visited Capri once after college to see my friend Angelina who lives here. I loved Capri then. But it seems so much more magical now."

He shot her a teasing grin. "That's because you're with me."

She laughed, a joyous sound that arrowed straight to his heart.

*****

They were quiet on the rest of the ride down to the center of Capri. Cat sank into the buttery leather seat and stared out the window at the raw beauty of Capri's cliffs and valleys. She could live here in this paradise with its perfume and flowers, surrounded by the calming waters of the gulf, and Vesuvius, a sleeping giant rising majestically over it all.

She slanted a glance at Alex. He gripped the steering wheel, his concentration on the road. His hawk-like profile and firm chin spoke of strength. She couldn't believe he could be a felon, but she had to know the truth.

Alex found a parking spot on one of the narrow side streets. With his hand on the small of Cat's back, he guided her along the cobblestones. The stilettos she wore made walking on the uneven streets difficult. She didn't care. She felt sexy and beautiful, even desirable.

And she'd relish every minute.

"The food at your parents' was good, but I didn't eat much," Alex said.

"Neither did I."

"Then, we will eat."

He led her to a small restaurant tucked away from the tourist mob. As they entered the courtyard where white-clothed tables were set out, a middle-aged man wearing a tuxedo came rushing from the interior of the restaurant. "Sandro, *amici miei*." He shook Alex's hand then turned a curious gaze to Cat.

"Ernesto, friend," Alex said in English. "This is *Signorina* Cat Connors."

Bowing slightly, Ernesto said, "*Buonasera, signorina*. Any friend of Sandro's is welcome here."

"Thank you," she said.

Ernesto rubbed his hands together, then snapped his fingers, summoning one of the waiters, who came running over. "Show my friends to their table. For my good friend and his lady, bring my best bottle of wine."

As they waited for their food and enjoyed the rich red wine, Cat flattened her palms on the table and leaned in. "Alex, I need to ask you something."

"Okay."

She swallowed, shoring up her courage. Now that she'd opened the door, she had to go through. "Before I left tonight, my father told me something disturbing about you. Is it true you might go to prison?"

Darkness shadowed his eyes but his gaze never left hers. "It is true."

Straightening, she gripped the table edge. "It is?"

"But I am not guilty. You must believe me."

"Everyone says they're not guilty. I want to hear your story."

He finished off his wine and plunked the glass back onto the table. A waiter hurried over and refilled his drink.

"My family owns diverse corporations all over Europe," he began. "I work for one of our financial companies in Rome. My father and uncle built it up from nothing. My father died several years ago, leaving me his shares of the company. I ran it with my Uncle Giuseppe and my cousin Camillo."

Alex raked fingers through his hair, messing it, then smoothing it over. He took a long drink of his wine and set the glass away from him. When he met Cat's gaze again, his eyes were flat as if drained of emotion. "Last year I discovered my uncle and cousin had been cheating our clients, much like your Mr. Madoff, for years. I urged them to return the money they'd stolen, but they wouldn't. I did the only thing I could. I reported them to the authorities."

Cat placed her hand over his on the table. "You did the right thing."

His bitter laugh hovered over them. "My family doesn't think so. We are to stick together and lie for each other if necessary."

"I'm sorry, Alex." She frowned. "I don't understand why you're in trouble with the law."

"My uncle and cousin planted evidence in our computers that implicated my father and me as the perpetrators of the crime." Alex's lips tightened into a thin line. "A judicial panel is reviewing the information now. I couldn't let my father's good name be destroyed.

I've been fighting to clear his name and mine, and to restore our company."

He grasped her hand. "It is important you believe me. Many of my friends have turned against me. Ernesto is one of the few who has been loyal."

"I noticed some of the guests tonight at Nolan's party snubbed you."

"I don't care about them. But I do care what you think of me."

The sincerity and hope in Alex's eyes and voice wrapped around her heart. "I believe you." And she did. She'd always had good instincts, and they were now screaming that Alex was telling the truth.

He released an audible sigh. "Thank you."

Waiters, followed by Ernesto, carried food to their table then. Alex freed her hand and they prepared to enjoy their meal.

The scrumptious dinner over, Cat put her napkin on the table. "That was the most amazing meal I've ever eaten, especially the gnocchi with fresh-shaved truffles."

Settling back in her chair, she sipped her wine. The meal had indeed been amazing, but not just for the food. They didn't talk again about Alex's legal or family troubles. Instead, he'd entertained her with stories of his childhood spent in his family's villa on Capri and at their apartment in Rome. His amusing stories made her laugh and warmed her like the elegant wine they'd shared. It felt good to laugh and forget she still had to deal with her stepfamily.

"I think your story about you and your cousin Vincenzo getting stuck on that hillside trying to rescue the goat was the funniest." She chuckled. "The goat walked away and you two were trapped there."

"Vincenzo and I always found creative ways to get into trouble. I'm an only child so he was like a brother to me."

She sighed with contentment. "Thank you for the meal. I'm going to suggest we serve gnocchi and truffles at the restaurant where I'll be working. I think it will be a hit." And she'd score points with her new boss by suggesting the luscious dish.

"Your family must be proud you are a chef," Alex said.

"Unfortunately, that's not the case." Cat pushed her empty glass aside. "My father wanted me to go into law and work for his company. My great-grandfather founded the firm. I wanted to please my dad so I went to law school and passed the California bar." She picked up her napkin and twisted the ends around her finger.

"The day I started at the firm, I applied to culinary school. I've always loved to cook, and the thought of sitting behind a desk all day to please my father broke something inside me. When I was accepted at culinary school, I gave up trying to earn my dad's love and acceptance. I finally grew up."

Alex's gaze softened. "Your father does not accept you or your choices? Family is very important. I have always tried to do what mine wanted, even convincing myself I loved the woman they selected for me."

Cat widened her eyes. "Your family chose a wife for you?"

"Sadly, yes."

"That's medieval. Who does that?" She winced.

"Sorry. I didn't mean to sound judgmental."

He gave a snort of dismissal. "It's okay."

Cat rested her elbows on the table. "What happened to the woman?"

"When my troubles started, she left me for a French race car driver in Monte Carlo."

"I'm sorry."

"Don't worry about me. You are much more *simpatico* than she was. I would rather be with you."

His words warmed her like the flame from the candle set in the middle of their table.

"You're very charming. You know that, don't you?" She wondered how much of his charm was real. Whenever he spoke to her, sincerity tinged his voice, and his clear eyes gleamed with intelligence and honesty.

"I like you, Cat. You are very sweet. And of course, beautiful."

She laughed. "Yes, you are *very* charming."

"Now that you know the truth about me, will you spend the day with me tomorrow? I'll show you more of my island."

She chewed her lip. There'd be no harm in spending time with him. "I'd love to."

CHAPTER FOUR

"I want to talk to you." The next morning, Bailey, wearing a tiny thong bikini that exposed her well-toned buttocks and barely held her implants, strolled onto the patio where Cat was finishing her breakfast. The rest of the family still slept.

Cat was glad she'd already eaten, or her appetite would have fled with Bailey's arrival. She threw her napkin onto the table and stood. "We have nothing to talk about."

Malice shot from Bailey's green eyes. "Stay away from Prince Sandro. A plain Jane like you can't handle him. He deserves someone hot like me."

Cat walked around the table and got in Bailey's face, invading her space. "Give me a break. First, he's not a prince. It's not a title he uses. His name is Alex and he's a nice guy. I like him. He doesn't belong to you. Now, if you'll excuse me, *Alex* will be here any minute. We have a date."

Cat pivoted on her heel and flounced out of the room.

As if on cue, the butler met her as she walked

through the dining room. "*Signor* Viteli is here for *Signorina* Connors."

Knowing she'd see Alex in a few seconds made her pulse jump up a notch, and she hurried out to the entry hall. Alex stood with his back to her. She stopped and admired his long, muscular form. Sexy and masculine in black jeans and a tan shirt, the sleeves rolled up to expose the fine golden hairs on his muscled arms, he oozed testosterone. Her mouth went dry.

As if he felt her watching, he turned slowly. Their gazes connected across the room. His hazel eyes darkened with something that took the breath from her. With the lithe grace of a lion, he strolled to her.

Bailey ran into the room and intercepted him, reminding Cat of a football player going in for the tackle. Bailey grabbed his arm and stared up at him while she licked her lips seductively. "Good morning, Sandro." She pressed one of her breasts against his arm.

"Morning, Bailey. Please call me Alex." With a bland expression on his face, he disentangled himself from Bailey's grasp and closed the distance to Cat.

"Cat." He kissed her hand. "You are the most beautiful woman on Capri."

With a loud grunt, Bailey stomped from the room.

Cat pushed Bailey from her mind, refusing to let the other woman ruin her day.

With a smile for Alex, Cat said, "I doubt I'm the most beautiful woman on Capri. Thank you for saying it though." His words heated her like sweet, warm honey. She did feel pretty in the tan silk capris and the pale blue sleeveless top that brought out the color of her eyes.

He skimmed a finger over her bottom lip. "You are very appealing," he said, his voice husky. "Any man who sees you will want you."

She shifted, unsure how to answer.

He placed his hand on her shoulder. "Ready?"

"Very."

His warm hand scorched her flesh, partially bared by her top. The way her body tingled at his touch, she was ready for much more than a sightseeing trip through Capri. Anticipation and a dollop of fear mixed a nervous potion in her stomach.

Once in the car, she asked, "Where are we going?"

Alex started the car and the Ferrari purred to life. "Have you been to the Blue Grotto?" He carefully maneuvered the car along the circular drive and onto the road.

"I went there when I visited Angelina years ago. It's such a tourist trap."

"With me it will not be a tourist trap. I guarantee it."

Cat settled into her seat. "Okay, then. Let's go."

*****

"Take my hand, *signorina*. Be careful." The middle-aged man dressed in a striped sailor top and faded jeans held out his hand to Cat.

She took the proffered hand and stepped gingerly into the small boat. Alex followed her, squeezing into the wooden seat next to her. They'd taken a motorboat crammed with tourists to the entrance of the Blue Grotto, then switched to this rowboat to go into the cave itself.

She moved over to allow Alex more room even

though they were the only two passengers. He draped his arm over her shoulders and drew her closer.

When they were settled, the sailor began rowing. "Young lovers," he said. "Capri is made for lovers."

"It is," Alex whispered in her ear.

Her insides churned with heady pleasure as their sailor guide ferried them toward the cave opening. While they waited their turn in the long line of tiny boats, the sailor explained that the Ancient Romans feared the Blue Grotto as the mystical dwelling place of monsters and spirits. The Roman Emperor Tiberius filled the grotto with statues and used it as his private swimming hole.

Although Cat listened in fascination to the legends of the Blue Grotto, a part of her was keenly aware of Alex's thigh pressed against hers. She'd been right about the grotto. It was touristy. Being with Alex made it exciting, sensual, and magical. She suspected he'd bring a vibrancy and excitement to even the most mundane things.

Finally, ducking their heads, they went through the low opening in the rock. Once inside, Cat straightened and gasped, filled with awe at nature's beauty spread before them. The water was a deep, glowing turquoise lit from below by phosphates. "This is amazing."

Their boatman began singing an operatic tune in Italian. Cat relaxed into Alex and let the beauty and the romance of the moment wash over her. On this enchanted island, in this mystical grotto with a thrilling, attentive guy at her side, she could allow herself to fantasize that she and Alex really were lovers. Cat's practical side dashed cold water on that thought.

She and Alex lived an ocean apart.

"Do you still think it is touristy here?" Alex placed a tender kiss on her temple.

She snuggled into him. "Not touristy at all, not with you as my guide. Thank you for showing me the *real* Blue Grotto."

He bent and touched his lips to hers. She closed her eyes and gave herself over to this exciting man in this magical place. Need and yearning coiled deep inside her.

"There is so much more I want to show you, Cat," he whispered against her lips.

Like the gentle mist of the grotto, his throaty voice enveloped her with the promise of romantic adventure.

They rowed around the grotto, one boat among many. Cat, wrapped in Alex's arms, felt as if they were the only two in this place of legends and otherworldly beauty, this place made for lovers.

Although their little sojourn ended too soon, and they were back on the island, the sensual enchantment of the Blue Grotto clung to Cat like caramelized sugar on crème brulee. She barely noticed the crowds pressing against them as they strolled hand-in-hand along *La Piazetta*.

Alex tugged on her hand and drew her into a narrow alleyway between two buildings. He gently cupped her shoulders and pressed her against the rough stone wall. "My Cat," he whispered in that low, sexy accent. "*Cara mia.*"

Her purse slid off her shoulder to land on the cobblestones. She wrapped her arms around his neck. "Alex." She released his name on a breathless sigh.

He brushed his lips over hers, slowly, tentatively, giving her the choice.

She savored his kiss, his scent of warm musk, his scorching touch. Heat licked her skin and traveled through her, igniting a flame low in her belly. His lips moved over hers, coaxing and teasing, inciting her to press closer, to seek his warmth.

When the tip of his tongue traced the line of her lower lip, she opened for him, craving his passion and his heat. Their tongues met in a primal dance. A volcano of need erupted within her. He did more than kiss her. He claimed her.

Awash in desire, Cat was in heaven and she never wanted to leave. When Alex threaded his fingers through her hair, a tortured moan escaped from deep within her.

He pressed his lips harder against hers, hot and intense. His tongue filled her mouth, exploring. Boneless, she melted against him.

Sounds, muted at first, then louder, penetrated her sensual bubble. In protest, she burrowed closer to Alex. She didn't want the magic to end, didn't want to leave the shelter and heat of his arms.

Children shouting out on the street brought Cat back to Earth with a thud. Her breathing rushed, she pulled away from Alex.

His eyes were glazed with want and desire. His skin stretched taut over his high cheekbones and his ragged breathing matched hers.

"Wow!" she said when she could talk.

He brushed his knuckles against her cheek. "*Carissima,* you are an amazing woman."

She placed a hand over her heart, feeling the pounding beat begin to slow.

"I've wanted to kiss you from the minute I saw you strolling down *La Piazetta*, lovely and sweet," he said.

"I-I wanted to kiss you too. Capri is like a love song. It makes people dream of love and kisses."

"It's not the island that makes me want you."

She swallowed. "Wow again. I need a drink." She bent to retrieve her purse.

He cupped her elbow. "We'll have drinks and lunch before I drive you back."

"Lunch sounds great." Afterward, back at the villa, she'd face the real world of Nolan, Tinsley, and especially Bailey. *Crap*. Thinking of the villa made her remember something, something she'd tried to forget. Cat pulled on Alex's arm, stopping him. "I forgot to mention this. When I got back to the villa last night, my dad and stepmother were waiting. I told them I was seeing you today, and they insisted you have dinner with us tonight."

"Then I will have dinner with you."

CHAPTER FIVE

Later, dressed for dinner, Cat studied herself in the beveled mirror in her bedroom. Her short skirt in varying shades of blue and her turquoise tank top enhanced the light tan she'd gotten since she'd been here. She hoped Alex would think her beautiful and that he'd kiss her again. Definitely kiss her again.

Before her mind could conjure up images of kissing Alex and a whole lot more, she exited her room and met her father coming out of the master suite down the hall.

He stopped and stared at her with an expression she didn't recognize. "Caitlyn, you look so much like your mother." His voice had softened.

"Thank you, Dad." She swallowed around the unexpected lump that formed in her throat. Her father held out his arm and Cat placed hers through his. Longing for what she never had, a father who adored her, pulsed through her.

Cat had long suspected her parents, who'd married very young, still loved each other. But her dad had cheated on her mom with Nolan. When Cat's mother discovered his betrayal, she threw him out, right into Nolan's arms. Knowing Nolan, and how miserable she made her dad, Cat felt sure her stepmother had seduced him into marrying her to elevate her social standing and her wealth. Not only did Davison Connors' family have money, they had platinum social credentials.

Her father had ignored his only child, and Cat didn't understand why. Growing up, the summers she'd spent on the Connors' family ranch in Napa, California, were filled with daily ridicule from mean girls Tinsley and Bailey and their wealthy, spoiled girlfriends. They liked to mock the no-label clothes Cat preferred.

Pushing aside the melancholy brought on by the painful memories, Cat plastered a false smile on her face and pulled her arm from her dad's as they joined the others in the spacious dining room. White curtains at the open French doors that led to the patio fluttered in the soft breeze and the scent of lemons floated through the room.

Entering this den of vipers, Cat squared her shoulders and prepared for battle. She hoped Alex would arrive soon.

Her father went immediately to the bar and poured himself a whiskey. Huntley was already there, a tumbler of whiskey in his hand. Tinsley, wearing a tight black strapless dress and black Roman-gladiator sandals, stood at his side sipping from a champagne flute.

Tinsley nodded at Cat, seemingly unaware that her fiancé's lecherous gaze trailed over her stepsister.

Cat took a glass of Dom Perignon offered by Paolo and walked to one of the comfortable chintz-covered chairs positioned around the room. The dining table, set for dinner, was white glass surrounded by modern chairs in chrome and white leather. The flowered chintz on the side chairs lent warmth to the cool room.

"Dinner will be served in ten minutes," Paolo announced.

Nolan, wearing a deep purple knee-length dress that showed her long legs, marched over to Cat. She bent to whisper in Cat's ear. "I don't know what game you're playing, but *Prince* Alessandro Viteli is better matched with Bailey. Leave him alone."

"Seriously, Nolan? You can't order me around."

Nolan's eyes sparked green fire. "You ungrateful little bitch. We'll see about that." She stalked away.

Shrugging, Cat sipped her drink. She felt as effervescent as the bubbling champagne. All these years she'd been intimidated by Nolan and her daughters. How freeing to no longer fear them or what they could do to her.

Bailey stepped into the room, wearing a tan sundress that fit her like a second skin. With a tight-lipped glare for Cat, Bailey grabbed a flute of champagne and flounced to sit at the other side of the room.

The doorbell rang, sending Paolo to answer it. A few minutes later, Alex sauntered in. His navy pants and crisp white shirt unbuttoned at the neck showcased his virility and style. He could have stepped from the pages of a fashion magazine, modeling the latest in couture for men. With his dark blond hair slicked back and a light stubble on his face, he could be a pirate on the cover of a romance novel.

His face broke out in a grin when he spotted Cat. Before he could take a step toward her, Nolan and

Bailey hurried to him, flanking him.

"Alessandro, thank you for accepting our invitation," Nolan said in a simpering voice.

Give me a break. Cat resisted rolling her eyes.

Bailey linked her arm through Alex's, one artificially enhanced breast pressing against his arm. Cat could swear Bailey batted her eyelashes.

Across the room, Cat's father watched with a frown on his face. Huntley and Tinsley, deep in conversation, ignored the others.

"Good evening, everyone." Alex extricated himself from the women and offered Nolan the wine bottle he held. "Thank you for sharing your meal with me tonight."

"How nice of you, Alessandro," Nolan said, taking the bottle from him.

"Please call me Alex."

When Nolan saw the label, her eyes widened. "Paradisio 2007 cabernet! This wine is very hard to get. The winery makes so few bottles a year that they're in high demand. How did you manage it?"

Alex lifted his chin. "My family owns the winery."

Nolan hugged the bottle to her ample chest. "How delightful to own a winery."

"Let me see that." Cat's father strode over and lifted the bottle from his wife. He read the label. "Yes, this is great stuff."

Paolo came into the room, followed by the staff bringing platters of food.

"Take this." Her dad handed the wine to Paolo. "Decant it. We'll have it tonight with the main course."

Nolan sat Cat as far from Alex as the table allowed.

Alex was pinned between Nolan and Bailey. If Alex was uncomfortable, he didn't show it. During dinner, his attention went often to Cat, and at one point, he held up his wine glass in salute to her. Alex beguiled them all with stories of growing up on Capri. Bailey laughed at all Alex's jokes, even the corny ones, and touched his hand constantly.

The meal over, the family congregated on the patio with after-dinner drinks. Nolan and Cat's father sat on chaises while Cat, Tinsley, and Huntley leaned against the bar. Bailey stood in the doorway with Alex, stuck to his side. When Cat met his gaze, Alex shrugged. Bailey tugged Alex over to a chair and tried to pull him down to sit next to her. He freed himself and strode to Cat.

"Take a walk with me, Cat?"

"I'd love to."

As Cat and Alex strolled down the marble patio steps to the outside, Cat could feel Bailey's stare, like daggers thrown at her back. Determined not to let Bailey intimidate her, Cat inhaled the calming scent of lemons mingled with the sweet perfume of roses and other flowering plants that grew in profusion on the vast estate.

Cat and Alex picked their way through the gardens to a narrow trail between high hedges. The trail led to a small cliff overlooking the Gulf of Naples. A white marble bench situated between two trees beckoned them. The gentle lap of the water in the gulf filled the air with a soothing rhythm.

They sat thigh-to-thigh. Alex's closeness and heat made warmth coalesce in Cat's chest and flow through her body.

She sighed. "Capri is an enchanted place. I wish I could stop time and make this moment last forever."

He took her hand in his. When she turned to him, his eyes were dark and mysterious in the pale moonlight.

"*You* are enchanting," he said.

His husky voice made her insides shake like unset soufflé. She looked deeply into his eyes and felt herself slowly falling over a velvet-lined cliff. "Alex."

"What do you want, Cat?"

She licked her suddenly dry lips. "I want you to kiss me."

He bent his head to brush his lips over hers in a whisper of a kiss that coaxed and teased. With a small moan, she pressed closer and opened her mouth, inviting his sensual invasion.

His deep, drugging kiss inflamed every cell in her body. She tunneled her fingers through the thickness of his hair and lost herself in Alex's heat, in the warm, spicy scent of him, in the promise of his lips.

Deepening the kiss, he cupped the curve of her jaw with his hand. Their tongues tangled. The heat of his body seared through the thin silk of her clothes. Desire and need, tempting and delicious as whipped cream on strawberries, settled in her stomach.

"*Carissima.*" His whispered word, filled with longing, made something deep and yearning stir in her.

He left her mouth to trail red-hot kisses down her throat to her collarbone.

She threw back her head in surrender. "Yum." The word escaped her.

She felt his smile against her throat. His fingers

skimmed the tops of her breasts, leaving a trail of fire in their wake as an ache built between her legs.

They sank together onto the bench, Alex leaning over her. He stared down at her with wonder in his eyes. Cat wrapped her arms around his neck and pulled him down to press her lips against his, drinking deeply of his passion and sensuality. Longing flared deep inside her.

"My Cat," he said on a tortured breath. When he bent to kiss her breast, she arched up and shivered at the sudden rush of pleasure.

"Cat! Alex! Are you out here? We're waiting on you for dessert." Bailey's strident, angry voice ripped apart the beauty and romance that had enveloped them.

Cat and Alex jumped apart.

With a wry smile, he stood and helped Cat up.

"Caitlyn! Alex!" Bailey's voice grew closer. "The gelato will melt if you two don't get in here."

"We'll be right up," Cat called out.

"Saved by gelato." Alex cupped her elbow as they strode back to the villa.

"I didn't want to be saved."

CHAPTER SIX

It was a wonder the homemade lemon gelato softened at all when she scooped some into her mouth, Cat thought, feeling the harsh, cold glowers from Nolan and Bailey. Cat sat in a chaise lounge on the patio, across the large expanse from the two women, with Alex on a chair next to her. Huntley sauntered over, and he and Alex engaged in quiet conversation. Tinsley, at the bar, was texting on her phone, seeming oblivious to the tension that hung over the room, heavy as lava from an erupting Mt. Vesuvius. Seated next to Nolan, Cat's father directed his scowls toward Alex.

Cat gave a mental shrug. Alex had made it clear he preferred her to Bailey. Her stepmother and stepsister would have to deal with it. Some of Cat's old insecurities kicked in, tightening her chest. A hot, attentive, and cultured guy like Alex actually wanted *her*, and not the more glamorous Bailey. No, she wouldn't think like that anymore. She'd worked hard these last few years to break free from her doubts and insecurities.

"Viteli." Cat's father cleared his throat, drawing everyone's attention. "Viteli, we know about your legal troubles."

Beside her, Alex released an audible breath. "They are common knowledge."

Her father sipped some of his whiskey. "Are you hiding out here on Capri?"

Alex stood. "I don't hide from anyone. I'm in touch with my lawyers every day. I assure you, sir, that I am innocent of all wrong doing."

Cat stood and touched Alex's arm, then focused on her father. "Dad, Alex is our guest. Nothing's been proven against him."

Nolan grabbed her husband's tumbler of whiskey from his hand. "Stop that right now, Davison. Alex is our guest."

"It's late," Alex said to Cat. "I should go." He nodded toward Nolan. "Thank you for dinner."

"I'll walk you out." Cat narrowed her eyes at her father as she and Alex headed out of the room.

*****

Tight-lipped, Alex left, followed by Cat. Davison Connors' words had cut.

"I'm sorry for what happened in there," Cat said when they'd reached Alex's car. The sincerity is her big blue eyes speared him with longing for love and acceptance. Gratitude that she believed in him swelled in his chest. He wanted to take her into his arms and never let go.

"It's okay. Your father is worried about his daughter. I would be the same. Thank you for defending me."

"He was being rude. I had to say something." She shook her head. "Odd that he would actually worry about me. He never seemed to care much about any guys I dated."

Alex leaned back against the car and pulled Cat with him, cradling her in the circle of his arms. "Tell me about your father and Nolan. Is your mother still alive?"

Cat splayed her hands on his chest, warming him through the fabric of his shirt. Her eyes met his.

"My mother is alive and well, and she's wonderful. She's an artist in Sausalito, California, outside San Francisco."

"I know that area. So your parents are divorced."

She nodded. "They divorced when I was three. Dad married Nolan soon after."

He settled Cat against his hip. "Nolan is an unusual name for a woman."

Cat chuckled. "Her real name is Mary. She changed it a long time ago. I guess she thought Nolan sounded more sophisticated than Mary." Cat shrugged. "Nolan's obsessed with social standing."

Alex frowned. "I assume your father and Nolan fell in love."

When Cat rested her head on his chest, Alex smoothed his hand over her hair, reveling in its softness. Soft and beautiful, like Cat.

"I don't know if Nolan and Dad have ever been in love." Cat's voice was muffled against his shirt. "My dad cheated on my mom with Nolan. My mother's not a woman to take infidelity from a man. She's not the type to take *any* crap from a man. She threw Dad out and Nolan was there to catch him."

"My poor Cat." He rested his chin on the top of her head.

She pulled away and gazed up at him. "It's okay now. I'm a big girl. Dealing with Nolan and her daughters was hard growing up, but I'm over it and I'm doing what I want."

"You and your father aren't close."

"Is it that obvious?"

He brushed stray locks of her hair back from her face, skimming his fingers over the creamy smoothness of her skin. "You're a loving, trusting person and I can feel the tension between you and your stepfamily. Your father seems to pay little attention to what goes on."

"You got it. That's my family."

"Your father is the loser because he doesn't know what a wonderful woman you are."

"Thanks, Alex." Her eyes glistened with tears.

Alex pulled her closer and kissed her waiting lips. Her sweet floral scent teased his senses. Images of taking Cat away with him, where the world couldn't intrude, flashed through his mind. But he couldn't run and he couldn't escape.

He sucked her full bottom lip and was rewarded with a low moan from her. She raked fingers through his hair and drew him closer. A door slammed somewhere and night insects cried out to each other, reminders that the world waited.

He reluctantly ended the kiss and gathered her against him. The rapid beating of her heart echoed his. He stroked her hair, wrapping silky strands around his fingers. "Goodnight, Cat. I will dream of you."

"Goodnight, Alex." She stood on tiptoe and brushed her lips softly over his.

Alex drove a little too fast along the winding roads

leading to his house on the opposite side of the island. Something in him craved Cat's freshness and needed her trust. Cat was different from most of the women he'd known. She was real and without pretense. Her goodness spoke to a part of his soul that had died when his family and fiancée abandoned him.

Prison and ruin loomed. He gripped the steering wheel, fighting the darkness that threatened his soul.

*****

Sunlight caressed Cat's eyes open. She stretched, welcoming another beautiful day on this bewitching island. A gentle, flower-scented breeze wafted through the open doors of her bedroom patio. Alex's face flashed through her mind. She rubbed a finger over her lips, remembering his kisses, his heat, his sensuality, and his tenderness the night before.

He'd awakened something in her, something hidden and dormant. She'd had relationships in college, one serious, with Ethan. Her ego had been bruised when he dumped her for another woman, but truth to tell, she'd been somewhat relieved. She and Ethan had had a comfortable relationship, with little passion. And Cat wanted passion. Especially after tasting it with Alex.

Later, dressed in shorts, a T-shirt, and flip-flops, she headed downstairs to breakfast. Only eight o'clock, she knew her stepmother and stepsisters wouldn't be up yet. When she entered the dining room, her father sat at the table reading *The New York Times.*

"Morning, Dad." She poured herself a mug of coffee from the pot on the sideboard. Setting the mug on the table, she helped herself to fluffy scrambled eggs, bacon, sourdough toast, and sliced melon. Nolan insisted on an American breakfast every morning. Cat had no idea how she'd managed to find sourdough bread on Capri.

Cat sat down, ready to dig into her food, when her father very loudly slapped his paper onto the table.

"What?" She met his harsh gaze.

"Are you ready to stop this nonsense?"

"What nonsense?"

His lips pulled into a thin line, and his eyes glinted with anger. "This whole rebellion thing you're going through. Aren't you a little old for this? Quitting law to be a cook! Now, consorting with a felon. Enough! When we go home, I expect you to come back to the firm."

Appetite gone, Cat pushed her plate away and wrapped her hands around her coffee mug, needing to control the trembling in her hands and stomach. "I'm not going back to law. It's not for me. And this 'rebellion' as you call it, is anything but. After years of trying to please you, and failing, I've given up. From now on, I'm doing what I want."

He winced as if stricken.

She gulped her drink, coughing a little as the hot liquid slid down her throat. Slamming the mug onto the table, she stood and stared down at her father, the man whose love she'd hungered for her whole life. Now, she saw him for what he was—a weak man who'd let himself be manipulated by a grasping social climber. A man without the guts to fight to win back the woman he loved.

She leaned closer until they were nose-to-nose. "I'm first sous chef at one of the best restaurants in San

Francisco. Someday I'll have my own restaurant. It's what I've always dreamed of. You wouldn't know that because you never bothered to find out what I wanted. And Alex is innocent until proven guilty. Nothing's been proven yet. I trust him."

"Caitlyn." He held out a hand.

She stomped away, proud of herself for standing up to him, for saying the things she should have said long ago. Her good feeling lasted until she got to her room. She threw herself on the bed and cried for the father she'd never had, for the death of her childish dreams that she and her parents would live together in their own happy-ever-after.

Cried out, Cat sat up and wiped the tears from her eyes. She was finally free to be the woman she always knew she could be. Through the years, her mother had tried to shore up her confidence, but Cat had been so intimidated by the mean-spirited treatment from Nolan and her daughters and by the benign neglect of her self-absorbed father, that she'd retreated into herself. No more. Her new clothes were the outward symbols of her self-assurance and freedom.

There was Alex. He made her feel desirable and beautiful. No one had ever done that before. She recognized his core of sincerity and goodness. He couldn't be guilty of any crimes.

Sadness rose in her. They lived an ocean apart. Nothing lasting would ever come from their brief flirtation on this magical island. She pressed a hand to her chest as if she could somehow touch her heart and soothe away the dull pain that formed at the thought of leaving Alex.

CHAPTER SEVEN

All that day, the villa bustled with workmen, caterers, and cleaning people, preparing for the huge party her father and stepmother were holding that night. Restless, wanting to see Alex and not wanting to spend another evening with Nolan's friends, Cat called Angelina to meet her for lunch. Friends since their undergrad days at Berkeley where Angelina, a native of Capri, was an exchange student, the two women had remained close.

Angelina drove to the villa to pick up Cat, and now they were seated at one of Capri's ubiquitous outdoor cafes finishing a lunch of yellowtail fish roasted on a bed of fennel with sides of fresh tomatoes and mozzarella cheese, topped off by espresso and strawberry kiwi gelato.

Cat patted her stomach. "I'm going to weigh a ton by the time I get home."

Angelina's brown eyes glittered. "I'm sure your Alex will think of imaginative ways to work off the pounds."

"Alex and I haven't made love. I barely know him."

"Ah, but you are falling for him. I see it in your

eyes." Angelina leaned forward. "Admit, it, Cat."

"Don't be ridiculous."

Angelina laughed. "You protest too much. I never saw your face light up when you spoke of Ethan the way it lights when you say Alex's name."

"I like him. Love? No way. Even if I did fall for him, we live in different countries. I have a new career, one I've worked very hard for. I won't leave San Francisco." She grimaced. "Once Alex's legal troubles are over, he'll have a ton of work to rebuild his company and his reputation. His life is here."

Angelina shrugged and picked up her wine goblet. "I have only met him a few times, but he seemed like a decent guy, not a playboy like some of his cousins. Very serious minded." Her lips tilted in a wicked smile. "He's hot too."

"Yeah, he is hot, and decent. I'd hate to see Bailey get her claws in him."

"I knew it! You are jealous of that bitch Bailey. She is nothing compared to you."

"I'm not jealous. I'm so over caring about Bailey and Tinsley."

Angelina touched Cat's hand. "Be careful of Bailey. She always seemed to have a meaner streak than Tinsley, even back in college. I suspect she's not changed. If she thinks Alex is hers, she may get nasty."

Cat snorted. "Bailey can't hurt me."

Cat's phone rang. When she saw Alex's name on the ID, she lowered her head to hide her grin from Angelina. She answered and struggled to keep the elation from her voice.

"Hi, Alex."

Across the table, Angelina thrust a fist in the air. "Yes!" she mouthed.

After a few minutes, Cat hung up to face a smirking Angelina.

"You *are* in love!" Angelina said. "Your face is lit up like the sun. He is coming here, yes?"

"Yes. We're going to spend the day together. He's close so he should be here any minute."

They paid the bill and headed out to the square to wait for Alex. When he arrived, he and Angelina exchanged hellos, then Angelina left, after getting reassurances from Alex that he would drive Cat home.

When they were alone, his hungry gaze devoured her. "You look good, Cat."

"Thanks." She felt good too, in the yellow cotton sundress and gold sandals. Cat hefted her large straw bag over her shoulder. "Where are we going?"

"I have a special surprise for you."

He took her hand, squeezing it as if he never wanted to let her go.

CHAPTER EIGHT

Alex held Cat's hand, helping her negotiate the cobblestones in her high heels. She took two steps to his every one. "Where are we going?" she asked again, glancing up at him.

Her sparkling eyes and the trusting way she held onto him made him want to taste her sweet lips, to protect her from her stepfamily, and give her the happiness she deserved. Facing prison, he had nothing to offer her. If exonerated, he'd spend the next few years rebuilding his business. Cat had her own life an ocean away. She was his today and he'd make her happy.

"We are almost there," he said.

He led her to a tiny lane, then up narrow stone steps to a walkway that overlooked the bay. As in the rest of Capri, flower-filled boxes lined the pathway. Quaint shops selling Limóncello, the sweet liqueur of Capri, couture clothes and shoes, and upscale household goods opened onto the walk.

"We're here," he announced.

They entered the tiny *perfumeria* filled with hundreds of perfume bottles of varying shapes and sizes.

"A perfume shop?" Cat said.

"The best *perfumeria* in Capri."

"Sandro!" Maria rushed from behind the counter and embraced him. Maria and her mother Lucia, along with Ernesto, had stood by Alex through his legal problems. They believed in him, and he would always remember their kindness. Their faith in his innocence gave him strength to keep fighting. He wanted Cat to know the people who'd remained loyal to him, unlike most of his family.

Maria shouted toward the beaded curtains. The beads tinkled like tiny bells as Lucia came out from behind them. When she saw Alex, she hurried over to give him a hug.

He took Cat's hand and pulled her forward, saying in English, "Maria, Lucia, this is Cat, my special friend."

Lucia grabbed Cat's free hand and said in heavily accented English, "We are always happy to meet a friend of Sandro's. He is a good man."

"I, too, am happy to meet a friend of Sandro's," Maria said with a welcoming smile.

Gratitude for his two friends sent a rush of warmth to Alex's chest.

"Come, we will make a perfume just for you." Maria waved a hand toward the work counter.

"Perfume for me?" Cat asked.

Alex nodded. "Maria will make a unique scent that no one else has. Every time you wear it, I hope you will think of me."

Her eyes wide and glowing with pleasure, Cat said, "That's so sweet. But I won't need perfume to remember you."

Alex wanted to take out his heart and hand it to her.

They walked to the counter where Maria was pulling vials from drawers. She poured tiny amounts of the contents onto small blotters for Cat to sniff. Most Cat rejected as too sweet or too heavy.

"I like these two," she finally said. "What are they?"

Alex picked up the vials and read the labels. "Lime and basil."

"Lime and basil? For perfume?"

"These two scents plus an added special ingredient will be perfect for you," Maria said.

Cat clapped her hands. "Cool! Thanks."

Lucia touched Alex's arm. "The perfume is our gift to your beautiful Cat."

"No, I will pay," he said.

"My mother is right," Maria said. "You are our friend. We help our friends."

"Thank you both." Alex's throat thickened. He owed these two, as he owed Ernesto.

Like a chemist concocting a secret formula, Maria mixed ingredients, then poured everything into a small blue crystal flask. She held it out to Cat.

Cat took the bottle and sniffed. "Oh. My. God. That is the best smelling perfume ever."

Maria laughed. "Try it now. Please."

Cat dabbed some of the perfume on her wrists and brought one hand up to take a whiff. She moaned softly. "Who knew lime and basil could be so heavenly?"

Maria sealed the bottle with a glass stopper, then put the flask into a blue satin bag and presented it to

Cat with a flourish.

"Thank you so much," Cat said. "I can't wait to wear this. It was wonderful to meet you."

With a sly grin, Lucia said, "We will meet again." She put a hand over her heart. "I feel it."

Hope sprang up in Alex. Lucia was known to be psychic. If only she was right, and Cat would someday come back to Capri and to him.

Waving goodbye to the women, Cat and Alex left the shop and sauntered leisurely back to *La Piazetta*.

Clutching the small pouch, Cat looked up at him. "Thank you for the perfume. I love it and I love that you wanted to give it to me."

He took her hand and pulled her to the side, away from the crush of the crowd. "I will never forget you, Cat." Ignoring the twinge in his chest at the thought of her leaving, he bent and kissed her lightly on the lips.

CHAPTER NINE

Sipping from small glasses of Limóncello, Cat and Alex sat on the balcony at one of Capri's best restaurants. They'd spent the day talking, laughing, sightseeing, people watching. The golden glow of the setting sun on the bay and over Vesuvius in the distance couldn't outshine the glow inside Cat.

"I'm so glad you called me, Alex. This has been a great day."

"Every day is great when I can see your beautiful face."

Despite his serious words, the glint in his eyes and his teasing tone made her laugh. She leaned closer. "One thing I like about you is that for a smokin' hot guy you don't take yourself seriously."

He threw back his head and laughed. "I love your American honesty." Settling back in his chair, he asked, "What else do you like about me?"

"Now you're fishing for compliments." She tapped her chin with her finger. "Let's see. I like how your English is perfect, especially since I don't speak Italian. I like that you make me feel good. I like that you're fun to be around. Is that enough?"

He frowned. "That's all?"

"That's all you're getting for now, mister."

Chuckling, he sipped his drink.

Cat checked the time on her phone and grimaced. "Damn. I need to get back. Nolan and Dad are having a party for their San Francisco friends who arrived today."

"Do you have to go to the party?"

She chewed her lip. "Not really. I doubt they'll miss me."

"Then stay with me. I'll make dinner for you. I want to hold onto you a little longer."

"You've made me an offer I can't refuse."

Thirty minutes later, they approached his villa. Cat's heart pounded when the white structure with the blue tiled roof that glistened with small white lights set around it came into view. A fairy-tale castle for a princess. Cat felt like Cinderella tonight, a casually dressed Cinderella. Was Alex her prince? A thoroughly modern prince, he hadn't returned her glass slipper but her phone. If this was her own private fairy tale, she'd enjoy it while she could.

Alex drove down a long driveway bordered by flowering shrubs and pulled up to the circular drive in front of the house. A bubbling fountain with a statue of Neptune surrounded by fish spewing water adorned the circle. Marble steps led to a large wooden front door painted red. A stone wall curved along the top floor of the house, and Cat guessed it offered a view of the bay.

Alex cut the engine, exited the car, and walked around to her side to open her door. Taking her hand, he helped her alight.

With his hand on the small of her back, he led her up the steps.

"Wow," she said when they entered the mosaic-floored entryway lit by large floor lamps set around the perimeter. In shades of deep blue and green, the floor mimicked the sea outside. Here and there, colorful fish seemed to swim between the undulating waves. "I feel like I'm floating in the ocean. It's beautiful."

"I'm glad you like it." He drew her close and kissed her, gently at first. His lips firmed over hers, hot and demanding. After several passion-filled minutes, he pulled away, his breathing ragged.

"First, we have dinner," he said softly.

"And after that?"

"Dessert."

"What's for dessert?"

"Whatever you want."

At the smoldering intensity of his eyes, a slow, simmering ache began to build in her. Cat pressed a palm to her stomach. Alex for dessert? She could handle that. "I'll help you with the meal."

Alex's large, open kitchen with its white cabinets, white tiled floor and dark blue granite countertops continued the feeling of floating in the ocean. French doors opened to a garden. The breeze brought the scent of roses. The center island looked out over the living room, furnished with modern, almost sparse furniture, with pops of blue and green, like underwater fish and fauna, among the sectional and chairs covered in white fabric.

She set her purse on a chair and headed for the

kitchen. "A chef's kitchen. Wow! A Wolf stove!" Feeling like a kid in a candy shop, she ran her fingers over the stainless steel of the six-burner stove with its double ovens. Turning to Alex, she said, "Wolf is one of the best, but why not an Italian stove, like a Bertazzoni?"

He shrugged. "Wolf is better. I prefer the best."

"You sure do." Widening her eyes, she took in the Sub-Zero professional-sized stainless refrigerator and the two side-by-side Asko dishwashers. With a kitchen like this, she'd probably never leave the house. She already felt at home here.

Despite the casual elegance and serenity of their surroundings, anticipation had Cat's whole body alert and waiting.

Alex began taking items from the refrigerator. When Cat saw the ingredients for antipasto, she said, "I'll make the antipasto."

While she put together the delicate lettuce, plump olives, fresh tomatoes, mozzarella, lean prosciutto, and sliced artichokes, Alex prepared the pasta to top with olive oil and fresh shaved parmesan.

As they worked side-by-side, Cat hummed along with the operatic tune playing on the radio. She'd cooked beside others countless times before, but never with this feeling of sensuality overlaid with contentment. She could get used to this life, here beside Alex on this island made for lovers. What a pleasant fantasy, but her real life was half a world away. Pushing aside the bite of sadness, she resolved to enjoy the here and now.

"We make a good pair," Alex said, mirroring her thoughts.

"We do."

He touched her nose with his finger. "You have some tomato on your nose."

She laughed. "I get food on me all the time."

He kissed her lightly on the lips. "You taste good. Like tomatoes and olives."

"I can't resist tasting as I cook." *And I can't resist you.*

They ate at the kitchen center island. The sauvignon blanc from Alex's family's vineyards complemented the light meal. With a contented sigh, Cat finished her wine and shook her head when Alex held up the bottle, ready to pour more.

Cat put her hand over her glass. "I've had enough wine. The meal, the setting, the company, everything was delicious."

"Are you ready for dessert?"

"Of course."

His lips curved into a slow, sexy smile. "What do you want for dessert?"

"You." The word slipped out. She surprised herself at her boldness.

At Alex's smile of delight, she cradled his face between her hands and kissed him.

He closed his eyes and drew a deep breath. When he opened his eyes, desire gleamed in them. "You're sure, Cat?"

"Very."

He took her hand and led her up the stairs. As they moved down a wide, dimly lit hallway, they passed bedrooms with open doors. Alex pulled her into a room at the end of the hall. A lamp set on a glass-topped table illuminated the large space. A king-size bed covered in dark blue dominated the room. Filmy white curtains fluttered from windows that opened to the sea breeze. The pale glow of the rising moon carved a path along the white tiled floor.

The scent of Alex's spicy cologne enveloped Cat as he took her into his arms. A surge of excitement shot through her. Giving herself over to the rush of desire, she wound her arms around his neck.

He tasted like wine and desire. Her stomach twisted into a knot of need. She parted her lips, wanting more of him.

Holding her, his mouth never leaving hers, he backed her up against the wall. She reveled in his groan of longing. Her body boneless, Cat melted against him, molding to his taut frame. She pushed aside the stirrings of doubt and fear that began to percolate within her. She would not think beyond this moment, with this man.

Alex trailed scorching kisses down her neck to the hollow of her throat. He cupped her buttocks and pulled her closer. His hard erection pressed against her.

"Cat." At her whispered name, intimate and raw with longing, something deep and yearning stirred in her. She skimmed her hands over his broad shoulders.

"I want to see all of you, my Cat," he said as he pulled away.

Swallowing around her dust-dry throat, she lowered the straps on her dress. Alex stopped her.

"I will undress you," he rasped.

He reached back and unzipped her dress, then tugged it to her waist. She felt the slight shaking of his hands as he unhooked her bra. Her bra and dress brushed her sensitized flesh as they slid to the floor.

Alex touched her face. "*Bellissima.*"

Then he turned his attention to her breasts. When he bent to take one puckered nipple into his mouth, she gripped his shoulders, afraid her legs wouldn't hold her. Trembling when he feasted on her breasts, she dug her nails into the flesh of his shoulders as the warm, wet pool of arousal soaked her panties.

He removed her panties. She stood before him naked. The sea breeze, bringing the scent of flowers, whispered along her skin. With unsteady fingers, she started to unbutton his shirt. He gently pushed aside her hands and quickly undressed.

Breathing heavily, she let her gaze roam over his exquisite nakedness. With his broad shoulders, muscled chest sprinkled with fine golden hairs, and long perfectly formed legs, he was a masterpiece carved in marble and come to life. The sight of his penis—large, throbbing and ready for her—sparked fire along her nerve endings.

Taking her hand, he led her to the bed. He yanked aside the comforter and drew her down onto the bed with him. Gathering her into his arms, he stroked her face, trailing his hand to her breasts. "Since the first time I saw you, I wanted you."

He rained kisses along her face and her jaw line. "My sweet, sexy, wonderful Cat."

She flung a leg over his hip and pressed closer, rubbing against his erection.

He groaned. "Keep doing that and I won't be able to control myself."

"I want you so much, Alex."

"Tell me what you want, what you like."

"You inside of me. Now. We have all night to do whatever we want."

"I like the way you think," he said in a thick voice.

He reached over to the small table next to the bed, opened the drawer, and pulled out a condom.

When he'd rolled on protection, Alex positioned himself over Cat. His eyes were dark, almost black, with desire. An answering need pulsed through her. She raised her arms, welcoming him.

He sank into her, moving slowly in and out, filling her completely. Her body tightened as shivers danced along her skin. Arching up to meet his every thrust, she wrapped her legs around his hips and ran her fingers over his back, digging her nails into his flesh.

His hungry kiss devoured her as his tongue filled her mouth. Her body on fire, Cat uttered tiny sounds of pleasure. Their bodies melted together as if made for each other, heart and soul fused. She belonged here with Alex, in his arms, a part of him.

Her climax built in waves that rivaled the sea outside. She nipped his shoulder, tasting the salt of his warm flesh. He hammered into her, faster and harder. Their groans echoed through the room. She screamed as her orgasm ripped through her. Alex stiffened, then shuddered. He called out her name as he climaxed.

Tears of joy welled in Cat's eyes.

Their breathing heavy, they lay wrapped in each other's arms. Finally, he rolled off her and settled her over him. Brushing hair away from her face, he tucked it behind her ears. The longing in his eyes tugged at her heart. "My Cat."

He pulled her head down for a tender, gentle kiss that captured her heart more surely than any words.

Cat pillowed her head on his chest and inhaled his unique scent mingled with the musk of their lovemaking. He wrapped his arms around her and held her tight.

In the security of Alex's arms, she'd finally found the acceptance and the belonging she'd craved.

Soon an ocean would separate them.

CHAPTER TEN

Alex put a hand over his eyes, adjusting to the sunlight streaming into the room. Beside him, Cat slept on her side, one hand tucked under her face. Propping himself on his elbow, he watched her, loving the way the sunlight brought out the red in her hair and the smoothness of her soft skin.

They'd made love into the early hours of the morning. A passionate woman who gave herself freely, Cat maintained an innocence, a wholesomeness that spoke to a need deep inside him, a hunger for trust and love.

Wanting her, he skimmed a finger down her face. She opened her big, beautiful blue eyes. Her smile reached into his heart and grabbed hold.

"*Buon giorno, cara mia,*" he whispered before kissing her full, inviting lips.

They made love again with a sweet desperation he'd never felt before. Holding her tightly, he wanted to imprint his body onto hers. Forever.

In a short time, she'd come to mean so much to him, but until his legal troubles were sorted out, he couldn't think of a future with her, couldn't think much beyond the next few days. He and Cat lived in different worlds, in different countries. He wanted her in his life and he'd find a way. He wouldn't be the man he was today if he gave up easily.

*****

Later, Cat, content and sated, sat with Alex on his patio drinking espresso and enjoying the breakfast she'd prepared.

Alex speared another forkful of spinach, mushroom, and potato frittata. "This is delicious, Cat. Almost as delicious as you."

She laughed. "Thank you. For both compliments. I think you're yummy too."

His laugh joined hers. "You're a great chef." He leaned closer. "And a sexy, warm-hearted woman."

Like the hot slide of the espresso down her throat, his words warmed her to her toes. She waved a hand. "You'll spoil me with all these compliments."

"I want to spoil you."

Images of spending her days and nights here with Alex rose in her mind. Reality poked through the romantic dreams. The real world waited beyond these walls. She grabbed his hand and squeezed it, wanting the dream to last a little longer.

CHAPTER ELEVEN

After breakfast, Alex drove Cat back to her family's villa. He concentrated on his driving, but his mind drifted to last night and this morning. She'd found a way into his heart and made him feel whole again. He glanced at Cat next to him in the car. Eyes closed, she rested her head on the back of the seat.

"Tired?" he asked.

"A little, but for all the right reasons."

Pleasure at her words heated him like the sun, already high in the sky. He gripped the steering wheel as he negotiated a tricky bend in the road.

"I wish we could spend the day together," she said. "But I have to get ready for the rehearsal dinner tonight." She touched his arm. "I'm so glad you'll be there with me."

"If it weren't for the chance to be with you, I would have politely declined Nolan's invitation."

He pulled up to the villa and parked the car, then turned to Cat. Cradling her face between his hands, he said, "I will miss you until tonight."

"I'll miss you too." She kissed him tenderly.

He wanted to peel out of there with her in the car, to take her somewhere the world wouldn't intrude.

"Alex." She sighed and touched his face. "I can't wait until tonight when I can see you again." She grabbed the handle and opened the door. "No need for you to get out of the car."

With the grace he found so appealing, she exited the car and ran up the steps. When she got to the top, she turned to wave at him.

Happiness, joy, and sadness formed a knot in Alex's chest as he drove away. He had a meeting with his lawyer today. Soon, he'd learn his fate.

*****

Surrounded by a cloud of euphoria, Cat headed to her room. The villa was quiet and she assumed the others were out. When she opened the door to her room, her happiness and feeling of goodwill fled out the window.

She gasped and stumbled to a stop.

Her beautiful clothes, her symbols of the new Cat, of her freedom, lay in tattered heaps on her bed. She dropped her purse on the floor. Dread pressed against her chest as she approached the bed. With a shaking hand, she picked up the orange silk dress she'd planned to wear to the rehearsal dinner. Someone had taken a scissor or knife to the beautiful fabric and shredded it until it was hardly recognizable as a dress. All her clothes had met the same fate, leaving Cat with only the clothes she now wore.

Tears sprang to her eyes when she spotted the lovely blue dress she'd bought for her mother. When she'd chosen the dress, she pictured her mother wearing it to one of her parties in Sausalito. Now, it was gone. Clutching the ripped blue dress to her chest, Cat sank onto the bed as tears streamed down her cheeks.

Who could have done this?

Angelina's warnings about Bailey shot into Cat's mind.

Bailey.

Red-hot anger propelled Cat from the bed. She threw the blue dress down and began pacing. Her mind conjured up images of ripping Bailey's clothes to shreds. She clenched her hand, imagining slamming it into Bailey's face. She'd rip out Bailey's hair too. She pictured those long blonde extensions on the floor.

Cat stopped in front of her dresser and gripped the sides as she stared into the mirror. She barely recognized the woman staring back, her face twisted in anger. She wouldn't let Bailey make her into something she didn't want to be. What was it her mother always said? "Living well is the best revenge" had been Molly Connors' motto. When Cat's father betrayed her mother with Nolan, Molly could have become a victim bent on revenge, but she'd made another life for herself. Cat prided herself on being her mother's daughter.

Angelina! She and Cat were the same size. Cat pulled her phone from her purse and punched in Angelina's number.

Cat would get back at Bailey in a way the other woman would never expect.

CHAPTER TWELVE

"Caitlyn! The limo is here," Cat's father shouted from downstairs. She snatched her evening bag from the bed and took one last look at herself in the mirror. Cat never wore red, yet Angelina's scarlet knee-skimming dress with the plunging neckline flattered her. Who knew she could wear red with her hair and coloring?

When she'd called Angelina earlier, her friend had rushed over with a variety of dresses and pants, saying Cat could keep them all. Cat owed Angelina big time.

"Maybe Cat isn't coming with us," Bailey said loudly enough for Cat to hear.

Cat exited the room and locked the door, then dropped the key into her purse. No one would get into her bedroom again. "Showtime," she whispered.

As she came down the stairs into the living room, the others were waiting, dressed and ready to get into the limo that would take them to the restaurant for the rehearsal dinner. Alex and the other guests would meet them there.

Bailey turned. The grin on her face disappeared

into a thin line. Her tanned face flushed. "Where did you get that dress?"

"Like it?" Fueled by a surge of adrenaline, Cat twirled. She swallowed the laugh that bubbled up. *Be cool, Cat.*

"You look beautiful," Cat's dad said. "As stunning as your mother." His voice had softened.

"Let's go." Nolan said, her voice strident.

Nolan wouldn't meet Cat's eyes, a sure admission of guilt from her always-composed stepmother. *Yes!* Cat had done it! She'd made Nolan squirm. Cat resisted the urge to thrust her fist toward the ceiling.

Putting a hand over her mouth to suppress her smile, she strutted to the limo, trailed by a sputtering Bailey.

Their large party took over a private room at the restaurant. Cat once again found her place at the opposite end of the long table from Alex. She sipped her wine and studied him over the rim of her glass. Elegant in a tailored black suit and white shirt, worn tieless and opened at the neck to reveal fine golden hairs, he possessed a sexy casualness most other men lacked.

He caught her gaze and winked. Next to him, Bailey placed her hand on his arm to draw his attention. With a shrug for Cat, he gently extricated himself from Bailey's grip, then started a conversation with the elderly woman next to him.

The waiters brought out the first course, antipasto made up of sausage, cheeses with honey and saffron, marinated vegetables, and bruschetta with olive paste.

During the rest of the courses which consisted

of linguine puttanesca, turkey breast with orange and greens, and biscotti with honey for dessert, Cat tried to focus on her conversation with the optometrist from San Francisco seated next to her. Her gaze kept drifting to Alex. A few times she saw him conversing with her stepsister. Bailey's too-big smiles when she listened to him contrasted to the rigidity of his posture and his unsmiling face.

The meal over, the guests relaxed with cappuccinos and espressos. Cat couldn't wait to escape from these stuffy people and be with Alex. She met his gaze and saw the question in his eyes. Her pulse kicked up.

The soothing scent of her lime basil perfume drifted up, a reminder of her night with Alex and what might come. Soft music played throughout the restaurant. Through the arched windows, the full moon beckoned. She was on Capri, a place made for love. She wanted Alex, a man who stirred her blood and made her long for something untamed.

When Alex gave her a barely perceptible nod, she lifted her espresso cup in acknowledgement. She'd go home with him tonight.

She lingered at the table as everyone started to leave. Bailey grabbed Alex's arm. When he tried to pull away, she flared her nostrils and shot an angry look at Cat. Alex managed to free himself. Bailey stomped off.

His gaze never leaving hers, Alex strolled up to Cat. He bent to place a tender kiss on her lips. "You will come home with me?"

"Of course."

They walked outside together and joined the other guests waiting for the valets and limo drivers to bring their cars.

"I need to tell my dad I'm going with you," Cat said. Alex nodded.

As Cat headed to where her father and Nolan stood waiting for their limo, Bailey gripped Cat's arm, stopping her. Eyes narrowed, Cat pulled away and rubbed her arm.

"What do you think you're doing with Alex?" Bailey spat out. "If you hadn't chased after him, he'd be with me. I told you he's mine."

Cat leaned forward. "That ship sailed a long time ago, Bailey. He's with me." She poked a finger into Bailey's chest. "If you ever destroy anything of mine again I'll forget I'm a lady."

When Cat reached her dad and Nolan, her stepmother regarded her with cold, flinty eyes. Nolan's lip curled. "What do you want?" she snarled.

Cat ignored her. "Dad, I'm going home with Alex. He'll bring me back to the villa."

"Do you think that's wise?" her father asked. "You're getting involved with this guy. What if he goes to prison? I don't want you hurt."

At the caring tone in her father's voice, emotion clogged Cat's throat. "I know what I'm doing, Dad. Alex is okay."

"Alex belongs with Bailey," Nolan snapped.

"Give it up, Nolan," Cat's father said.

"Thanks, Dad." A smile played around Cat's mouth as strode briskly back to Alex, almost skipping in her elation.

CHAPTER THIRTEEN

The next morning, Cat stood at her bathroom sink and splashed water on her face. With Tinsley's wedding in an hour, she had to hurry. Her body, still languid from a night spent in Alex's arms, didn't want to cooperate.

Clutching the edge of the sink, she stared at herself in the mirror. Alex had driven her back thirty minutes ago. Although she'd gotten very little sleep the night before, she didn't feel tired. Just the opposite. She looked and felt...rejuvenated. Her face seemed to glow and her eyes sparkled. Alex did that to her.

She'd fallen in love with him.

Crap. She turned around and leaned against the sink. No, no, she couldn't be in love. Not now.

She belonged in San Francisco. Alex had to stay in Italy.

What the hell could she do? If Alex didn't return her feelings, her heart would break, but that would make going home easier. Even if he felt the same way about her, he might be going to prison. No, she couldn't believe that.

She and Alex had no future.

Hollowness settled in her chest.

*****

Later, sitting in one of the white wooden chairs set up in the gardens, Cat waited for Tinsley's wedding to start. A white carpet had been laid down between the two rows of chairs. In front of the chairs stood a small platform topped by a lattice-worked arch decked with flowers where Tinsley and Huntley would take their vows.

Cat smoothed a hand down the pale blue silk dress Angelina had given her. The strapless dress molded to her body as if made for her. Thankfully, Bailey hadn't destroyed Cat's shoes. The silver stiletto sandals she wore were her favorites. She'd needed very little makeup today. The light tan she'd gotten and Alec's lovemaking gave her a natural glow.

She'd see Alex soon. Contentment, sweet as the richest chocolate, settled in her chest. She twisted in her chair to watch the other guests taking their seats. Alex must have gotten delayed. He'd promised to be here early. She spotted him, standing in the entry to the garden. Cat stood and waved. Alex's bright smile sent a surge of happiness through her.

As he made his way over the white carpet, she admired his long, lithe body. Most men looked good in a tux, but Alex took it to a whole new level. Sophisticated and elegant, with a sexy grace, he could have walked out of a magazine ad for Armani. Heads turned as Alex passed by. A few people whispered to each other, and Cat wondered if they talked about his family's legal problems or his extraordinary looks.

When Alex got to her, he bent to kiss her lightly on the lips then took the seat next to her. "You get more beautiful each time I see you." He grabbed her hand and held it. "That dress is perfect on you."

"Thanks." She hadn't told him about Bailey destroying her clothes, and she didn't intend to. She'd handled it. Giving him a flirtatious smile, she said, "You sure know how to fill out a tux."

He laughed. "Thank you."

The music started, *Triumphal March* by Grieg, played by a violinist. The Italian official who would perform the ceremony took his place on the flower-bedecked platform.

Nolan, dressed in shimmering silver, walked down the aisle on the arm of one of the groomsmen. Next came Huntley's parents. Huntley appeared from the side, accompanied by his best man. They took their places on the platform.

The guests stood, their attention on the garden entrance. Bailey, the maid of honor, wearing a pale green faille dress walked slowly along the carpet. Her scowl and her pouting lips marred her pretty face. When she'd taken her place at the front, Tinsley, on Cat's father's arm, floated down the aisle, a vision in couture and heirloom lace. The gasps from the guests voiced their approval of the stunning bride in an ivory Valentino gown that draped perfectly over her curves.

A short while later, the ceremony over, the guests moved to a large tent that had been set up under a grove of lemon trees. Cat, on Alex's arm, inhaled deeply. The scent of lemons and roses would always remind her of Capri. She glanced at Alex. Capri and Alex would always be entwined in her heart.

After appetizers and drinks, and mingling with the other guests, Cat and Alex sat down for dinner at a table with her dad and Nolan. The tension flowing from Nolan was heavy enough to cut with a serrated knife. She barely acknowledged Cat and Alex. Cat's father tried to make conversation, but eventually an uneasy silence settled over them.

Alex grabbed Cat's hand under the table and squeezed. She squeezed back and began to relax. With Alex beside her, she'd get through this day despite the anger shooting at her from Nolan and Bailey.

The photographer motioned to Cat's father and stepmother that he wanted to take their picture, leaving Cat and Alex alone at the table. As they were enjoying their lobster and filet mignon, the steak so tender it could be cut with a butter knife, Bailey left the wedding party table and strode to theirs. She leaned close. Malice flashed from her eyes.

"This isn't over, Cat," she hissed.

Cat twisted her fingers around her fork. "Grow up, Bailey."

"What's going on?" Alex asked.

Bailey fixed him with an angry glare and waved a hand over her voluptuous body. "You gave up all this for a skinny cook?"

Alex stood. "Cat is beautiful inside and out, and a talented chef. I'm honored to have her in my life."

His sweet words and the way he rushed to her defense brought a smile to Cat's lips. Beyond Bailey's shoulder, Cat could see the photographer assembling the wedding party. Tinsley called out to Bailey.

"You're wanted elsewhere, Bailey," Cat said.

Bailey's face reddened and her lips curled. With a snarl, she stamped away.

"What was that about?" Alex asked when he'd sat down again.

"It was nothing," Cat said. "Just Bailey being Bailey."

Alex's brow furrowed. "You're sure?"

"I'm sure."

Night had fallen by the time the four-course meal finished. A wooden dance floor had been laid next to the lemon grove. During dinner, the band had played soft music, and now played a rock tune that got many of the guests up and dancing.

Alone again with Alex at the table, Cat settled back in her chair. The scents of flowers and lemons floated on the gentle breeze and night insects sang among the bushes and shrubs. A perfect night, one made for love. She was with the perfect man, handsome, intelligent, kind, and sexy.

Alex took her hand and threaded his fingers through it. "It is a beautiful night," he said, as if reading her thoughts.

"It is." She kissed him lightly on the lips.

The band struck up a romantic ballad.

"Dance with me?" Alex asked.

Holding hands, they sauntered out of the tent to the dance floor. Cat lifted her face to a sky sprinkled with stars, with small clouds scudding by like sailboats on the tranquil bay. When Alex took her into his arms, Cat rested her head on his chest and allowed him to lead her in a slow, sensuous dance. The other dancers faded away until only the music, the starry night, and the man who held her close filled her senses.

"Your perfume suits you," Alex said. "Sexy, sweet, and innocent."

Cat lifted her head to meet his eyes. "A very dear man gave it to me. Someone who means the world to me."

"You mean everything to me." Alex bent his head to lightly touch his lips to hers.

The power of his words made Cat's body tingle with joy. She had a vague sense of the music ending, but she and Alex continued to sway, their bodies so close they moved as one. Soft clapping and a few whistles stirred her from her dreamy haze. They pulled apart to see others watching them, grins on their faces. With a laugh, they bowed to the crowd, eliciting more clapping.

As they strolled leisurely back to their table, their arms around each other's waists, Alex leaned down to whisper in her ear. "Let's leave. Come home with me?"

"Yes," she whispered.

CHAPTER FOURTEEN

As dawn broke over Capri, Cat, unable to sleep, stared at the ceiling and snuggled closer to Alex. Their lovemaking had been passionate but spiked with an underlying sadness. Her time on this enchanted island had almost come to an end.

"You are awake?" Alex said, his voice heavy.

She rolled to face him. "I couldn't sleep. Too much on my mind."

He brushed strands of hair back from her face. "What is bothering you, my Cat?"

Skimming a finger along his full bottom lip, she said, "I don't want to leave Capri. Or you."

He sat up and pulled her with him, settling her against his chest. "Don't leave." He stroked her hair. "Stay here with me."

"You know I can't. My home and my life are in San Francisco. For the first time, I'm free to follow my dream, to see where it takes me." A tear slipped down her cheek.

Alex gathered her closer and rested his chin on the top of her head. "I understand, but I need you. Every day I have you in my life, my world is brighter. With you I have hope. I love you, Cat."

Wiping away her tears she pulled back and met his gaze. "You love me?"

"You must know I do."

"I'd hoped, but..." She let her voice trail off.

His eyes lit. "You love me?"

Her throat thick, she could only nod.

He cupped her jaw. "I don't want to lose you. I can't offer you anything until I learn my fate. When my legal problems are over, we will find a way to be together."

Pierced by a poignant ache, Cat smoothed a hand over the sharp planes of his face, the chiseled cheekbones, the full lips, and the firm chin, committing the look and feel of him to memory. "We live so far apart. I've fought hard to have the career I want. I can't walk away."

His features stark, he drew a deep breath, as if fighting for control. "I can't leave Italy, even if I'm exonerated. There will be much work for me to do."

"I don't want a two-continent love affair. I don't see how—"

He put his finger over her lips. "Shush. I love you, Cat, more than I've ever loved anyone. Things will work out. They must work out."

She wanted to believe him, but reality reared its head. She couldn't see any way she and Alex could be together.

He kissed her, deeply, tenderly. She clung to him. Their lovemaking was slow, gentle, and tinged with melancholy.

*****

Later, her stomach heavy as if a rock had settled

there, Cat entered her family's villa. Her father waited in the living room, pacing.

"Hello, Dad."

"We need to talk, Caitlyn."

Her shoulders sagged. "Okay. Come up to my room."

When they entered her room, she closed the door and leaned against it, facing her father. His skin was ashen under his tan.

"Are you okay, Dad? You look sick."

He raked a hand through his thick gray hair. "I'm not physically ill."

"Let's go onto my patio. I think we can both use the fresh air." She took a seat at the white iron table. Her father leaned against the railing and met her gaze.

"Do you love Viteli?" he asked.

"Yes."

"He could go to prison."

She blew out a breath. "I know, but I believe in him. I think he'll be cleared. Alex is an honorable man."

"I don't want you hurt."

"You never seemed to care about me before." The words spilled out.

Her father flinched as if she'd hit him. "I deserve that." He scrubbed a hand over his face. With a heavy sigh, he dropped his hands to his sides. "I've always known Nolan and her daughters treated you badly."

Cat gripped the sides of her chair. "Why didn't you stop them?"

"Because I'm a weak excuse for a man. I made a terrible mistake when I betrayed your mother. I've suffered for it every day since. Through my own arrogance, I lost the only woman I ever loved. My guilt has been so encompassing that looking at you is a reminder of what a fool I've been. So I ignored you and used alcohol to forget. I broke your mother's heart and I let you down."

"All I ever wanted was your love." Tears burned her throat but she refused to cry. She'd done enough crying today. Her father had broken her heart too.

In two strides, he knelt before her, taking her hand in his. "You have my love. You've always had it. Can you forgive me, Caitlyn?"

She curled her free hand into a ball to stop herself from touching his face. "I need time, Dad. A lot of years and a lot of heartbreak stand between us."

With a defeated sigh, he released her hand and stood. "I get it. I'll work hard to earn your respect if not your love." His eyes searched hers. "Be careful with Viteli. If you need someone to talk to, I'm here."

"Thank you, Dad."

With a last, tortured look, he walked out. Regret for the lost years and hope for the future made Cat's tears flow freely.

Not wanting to see the others, Cat took her dinner in her room then packed. She stacked the clothes Bailey had destroyed in a bundle on the floor. All her hard-earned money, all those beautiful clothes gone. And for what? Clothes weren't important. Love and trust and respect were. Maybe she'd have that someday with her father.

Alex already had her trust, her respect, and her heart.

Packing done, she was dressing for bed when her

phone rang. Seeing Alex's number, her fingers fumbled as she connected the call.

"Alex." Her voice was breathy.

"I have good news. I've been cleared."

The elation in his voice sent shivers of happiness up her spine. "That's wonderful! I knew it! I knew you'd be cleared." She sank onto her vanity stool.

"The judicial panel reviewed the records and dismissed the case for lack of evidence," he continued. "The judge called my lawyer personally this morning to tell him. My lawyer drove down here to give me the news. The authorities are initiating an investigation of my uncle and cousin for presenting false statements."

"Alex, I'm so happy for you."

"You always believed in me, Cat. I will never forget that."

Her chest tightened and her limbs felt heavy. Alex's words sounded like goodbye. "What happens now? With you and with us?" She had to ask the question, but she dreaded the answer.

"Cat." His voice had softened. "I love you and we will be together. I promise. Right now, I must leave for Rome."

She heard a man's voice in the background.

"My lawyer is telling me the ferry to Naples is ready to leave. We have a long drive from there to Rome. I will call you every day, my beautiful Cat. Please have faith in me. I love you."

"I love you too."

Cat ended the call, threw the phone on the bed, flopped down onto the white comforter, and let the tears come again. Her happiness for Alex mixed with fear, churning an anxious brew in her stomach. He said he loved her, and she believed him. He'd needed her when things had looked dark. Now that he had his life back, maybe he would no longer need her. Or love her.

CHAPTER FIFTEEN

"Stir the gravy gently, like this, Yvette. It won't be lumpy." Cat took the wooden spoon from the young cook and demonstrated the correct way to blend the distinct gravy that would go on the pork loin, a specialty of Vault. Taking a small spoon, she ladled out some of the gravy and tasted it. "Very good."

The young cook beamed and took over the stirring duties. "Thanks, chef."

Cat focused her attention on the braised veal, putting on the finishing touches before the server brought it to the customer. She wiped sweat from her forehead with a towel. She never got tired of being called "chef." Although the celebrated Bobbie St. James ran the kitchen, Cat held the position of his top sous chef. Across the busy, noisy room, Bobbie consulted with one of the young cooks.

Cat had left Italy and Alex one month ago. Her fears that distance and the end of Alex's legal troubles would undermine their fledgling relationship lessened with the daily calls and texts they shared. He always called to say good morning as her day was starting and his was drawing to a close. He ended each call with, "I love you." Whenever she heard his voice, ecstasy bubbled up in her, tempered by sadness because she missed him so much. Their time apart made her love him more, and appreciate him more. He'd earned her respect too with the hard work and long hours he put in sorting out the mess his uncle and cousin had made to his company.

Cat understood about dedication to a career. She worked long, sometimes grueling, hours at the restaurant. The work filled her days, and her nights were filled with dreams of Alex, his smile, his laugh, his kindness, his sensuality.

Fighting waves of loneliness for him, she gripped the edge of the counter. She hadn't heard from Alex in two days, despite sending him several texts. The comforting aromas of onion, garlic, oregano, veal, and pork that enveloped her failed to take a bite out of the worry that ate at her. She inhaled sharply, breathing in the lime and basil of the perfume Alex had bought her on Capri. Wanting to make it last, she wore it sparingly. This morning, as she got ready for work, missing Alex fiercely, she put on the perfume as if it could bring him closer.

The Thanksgiving and Christmas holidays were approaching, the restaurant's busiest season. After the holidays, they would close for two weeks for some minor renovations. This morning, Cat decided she'd go to Italy during the break. She had to see Alex. If only he'd call to reassure her everything was okay.

The clatter of broken dishes shattered her thoughts. The murmurs of conversation in the kitchen died as all eyes focused on the red-faced busboy who'd dropped a tray loaded with dirty dishes. Cat hurried over to reassure the poor kid while one of the prep guys grabbed a broom.

The temporary crisis over, Cat pulled a salmon filet from the refrigerator. As she set it on the prep counter, Edward, the maître'd, rushed in.

"Cat, there's someone here to see you," he said.

"See me? Does he have a question about his meal? I've got to prepare this salmon."

Edward shook his head. "He didn't eat here. Just now walked in."

She glanced over at Bobbie. "Go ahead, Cat," he said. "I'll get one of the other sous chefs to take over."

In front of the door, she slipped off her skull cap, loosened her hair from its low knot and raked her fingers through it, letting it fall over her shoulders. Smoothing the chef's jacket she wore over her skirt and sweater, she went through the swinging doors into the dining room.

And froze. Her legs as wobbly as watery gelatin, she backed up against the wall as her heart beat a wild staccato.

Alex, holding a large bouquet of red roses, stood across the room. Dressed all in black—black jeans, black turtleneck sweater, black leather jacket, his dark blond hair brushing against the collar of his sweater— he looked like a tasty dessert she wanted to devour.

His gaze never leaving hers, he walked slowly across the room and handed her the roses. "For you, my beautiful Cat."

With shaking hands, she accepted the flowers and

buried her nose in them. Taking a moment for her mind to settle, she inhaled their sweetness. She lifted her gaze to his. "Alex. You're here." *Way to state the obvious, Cat.*

"I couldn't stay away."

Cat set the flowers on the bussing table near the door and walked into Alex's arms, clinging to him, afraid if she let go she'd realize he'd been an apparition conjured up by her loneliness.

He pressed her close and stroked a hand down her hair. "Cat. Cat." His husky voice, filled with yearning, warmed her like rich Italian coffee.

Finally, he pulled away and cupped her face between his hands to look deeply into her eyes. "I must talk to you."

Her breath caught at the serious tone of his voice. He wouldn't have come all this way to break up with her. "I don't get off work for hours yet."

Someone nearby cleared his throat. Behind her, Edward hovered.

"Bobbie says take as much time as you want with your *friend*," Edward said.

"Tell him thanks." Cat grabbed Alex's arm and tugged him to a small empty table in the corner. In a poor location, the table was occupied only when the rest were filled.

When they sat down, Alex grasped her hand over the table. "Cat, you are *molto bellisima*."

"So are you."

He threw back his head and laughed. "I have always loved your American honesty."

She narrowed her eyes and tilted her head in mock

outrage. "Talking about honesty, why didn't you tell me you were coming? I could have been prepared and at least taken off my chef's coat. You haven't called in two days. I was worried."

"Clothes mean nothing. You are beautiful no matter what you wear." A wicked gleam in his eyes, he added, "Or don't wear."

"You're sweet." She grinned. "And sexy. You always know the right thing to say."

"I would like to be very sweet and sexy with you every day and night." He released her hand. "I didn't mean to worry you. I have been especially busy these last few days, tying up things at the company and preparing for this trip." With a tender smile, he continued, "I was afraid if I spoke with you on the phone, I'd tell you I was coming here. What I need to say, I must do in person."

Cat put a hand over her stomach, pressing to stop its trembling. "What do you have to say—?"

A waiter carrying a bottle of champagne and two glasses interrupted. "The staff sent this over."

When he'd filled their glasses and left, Alex raised his. "To my lovely Cat."

She touched his glass with hers, sipped, then set down her glass. "Alex, what is so important you had to tell me in person? And how were you able to get away from your work?"

"The company is in the very capable hands of my cousin Vincenzo." He leaned closer. "I have a surprise for you."

At the happy glint in his eyes, hope rose in her. "Surprise?"

With a satisfied smile, he leaned back and wrapped

his fingers around the stem of his champagne flute. "With Vincenzo's help, things are coming along at the company better than I'd hoped. Most of my family has forgiven me for calling the authorities when I found out what Uncle Giuseppe and cousin Camillo were doing. The Italian press has been kind and my father's good name is almost fully restored."

"Alex, that's wonderful news."

"There's more."

"What else?"

"I'm selling my shares in the company to Vincenzo. He'll build it up to what it once was."

Cat sat straighter and touched Alex's forearm. "Are you all right with that? You sacrificed a lot for your company."

"To continue to run it would mean I would have to stay in Italy. I know how much your career and this restaurant mean to you. You worked hard and I can't ask you to give that up." He placed his hand over hers where it rested on his arm. "If I have to sell my company to spend my life with you, that's a small sacrifice. Without you, my life is dark and without meaning. With you so far away, I realized how much I need you and love you."

Her breath came in small gasps. "What-what are you saying?"

"I am moving to San Francisco. A financial company here has been trying to get me to work for them. I've accepted their latest offer."

When she didn't speak, he frowned. "Maybe you no longer want to be with me."

The shock that had frozen her voice melted. "Oh. My. God. Alex, I love you so much. You'd do this for me?"

"Of course. Why wouldn't I sacrifice to be with the woman I love?" He slipped a hand into his jacket pocket and pulled out a small jewel box.

Cat forgot to breathe.

He slid off the chair and knelt on one knee on the floor in front of her. "Caitlyn Megan Connors, will you marry me?" He opened the box. Inside, on black velvet, rested a marquis-cut diamond ring. The facets of the large gem sparkled in the overhead lights. "It was my grandmother's. I would be honored if you would wear it."

Tears streamed down Cat's face. "Yes, of course I'll marry you. Yes!"

Clapping broke out in the restaurant.

Alex took her hand to help her stand. He slid the ring onto her finger. It fit perfectly.

She threw herself into his arms. With her right arm around his waist, she held her left hand out, admiring the ring. "I love it! How did you know my size, and how did you know my middle name?"

"I called your mother."

"My mother?"

"I had to get her permission to marry you. She's here." He nodded toward the door where Molly Connors, her face tear-streaked, waited.

Molly ran across the room as the guests and wait staff clapped and cheered. The two women embraced. Alex hugged both women.

A beaming Edward came over. "We have a table reserved for you. Bobbie has prepared a special meal to celebrate."

Cat's eyes met Alex's. "You arranged all this?"

"But of course."

Holding onto his arm, she said, "It seems like a celebration is in order."

His eyes softened. "I will celebrate every day you are mine, Cat."

She'd not only found her true self on Capri. She'd found a true love to last a lifetime.

EPILOGUE

Capri, ten months later

Canon in D by Pachelbel, performed by a cellist, filled the small mountaintop church. Guests, seated in their pews, fidgeted, waiting for the ceremony to start.

Cat, flanked by her parents, stood in the vestibule of the church.

"Ready?" Molly Connors said to her daughter.

Cat's hands holding her wedding bouquet shook. "As ready as I'll ever be."

"You're the most beautiful bride I've ever seen, with the exception of your mother," her dad said. Tears rimmed his eyes.

Her parents each threaded their arms through hers, preparing to walk her down the aisle.

A soprano from one of Italy's top opera houses took her place in the front next to the cellist. Alex and his cousin Vincenzo, his best man, entered from the side and stood next to the priest at the altar. The guests quieted now, excitement in the church palpable.

Cat's gaze met Alex's across the expanse. The

happiness that surged through her made her heart drum against her chest and echo in her ears. She held the bouquet tighter, fighting the temptation to fling it aside and run down the aisle to jump into Alex's arms. As if he read her mind, he winked.

The soprano, accompanied by the cellist, began singing the soaring strains of Schubert's *Ave Verum*.

Arm-in-arm, Cat and her parents walked down the white-carpeted aisle. Cat barely noticed the others in the pews. She had eyes only for her handsome groom. The custom-made tux enhanced his wide shoulders and broad chest. His dark-blond hair was slicked back, emphasizing his high cheekbones and full lips. But it was the love shining from his hazel eyes that made her breath catch and her feet falter.

At the altar, her parents stepped aside. Her dad took his place in the first pew, and her mother stood next to Cat as her matron of honor.

"Cat," Alex whispered, as he took her hand. "*Molto bella.*" Together, they turned to the priest.

Her mind in a blur, the priest's voice barely registered. Then came time to recite their vows, vows Cat and Alex had written together. She handed her bouquet to her mother.

Holding hands, Cat and Alex faced each other. Her gaze never leaving his, Cat began, "Alex, you are my heart, my life, my soul. You make me happy. You make me laugh and smile. The day I stepped onto this island and met you, my life changed. You've opened a new world of love to me. You're my rock, the man whose face I want to see each morning and whose lips I crave each night. I want to have your children, grow old with you, and tell you every day how much you mean to me. Will you brighten my days forever?"

Beside her, her mother sniffed.

"Cat, the day I saw you walking along *La Piazetta*, sweet and filled with life, I lost my heart to you. You are beautiful inside and out. Fate brought us together to laugh and smile and build a life. You are the person I want to share everything with. I will spend every day making you as happy as you've made me. I will cherish you and the children we will have. We will brighten each other's days forever. Will you take my ring as a pledge of our love? You already have my heart."

Cat's mother sniffed louder.

With a wicked grin, Alex leaned in and said loud enough for the others to hear, "If I hadn't been watching you so closely that first day, I wouldn't have seen you drop your phone. It was my lucky day."

Returning his grin, she said, "Well, this Cinderella doesn't need a glass slipper, but she sure needs her phone. I'm so glad you returned it."

Laughter erupted in the church.

When the laughter died down, Alex's best man handed him the diamond studded wedding band. Alex slipped it onto Cat's finger. "Wear this ring as a symbol of our enduring and passionate love."

Her mother handed her the plain gold band that would be Alex's. Cat slipped it onto his finger. "Wear this ring as a symbol of our enduring and passionate love."

Happiness covered Cat like sweet melted butter. She was afraid her heart would burst through her chest.

The priest said prayers over them, then pronounced

them husband and wife. They walked swiftly down the aisle to smiles and claps. Her father had tears streaking his face.

*****

Cat leaned against Alex as they stood on the upper balcony of his villa overlooking the calm turquoise waters of the gulf. She breathed in the heady scent of flowers that grew over the walls of the balcony, in a riot of colors, dancing in the setting sun. She lifted her wrist to take a whiff of the lime basil perfume, a scent that would always remind her of this enchanted island and the man who'd captured her heart.

"Happy?" Alex drew her closer and kissed the top of her head.

"Very." She smoothed a hand down the ivory silk of her elegant wedding gown, a one-of-a kind dress designed by her mother. "I wish all these people would leave so I can get you into bed to ravish you."

He laughed. "How can we make them go away?"

She scanned the gardens below where white-clothed tables had been set up for their wedding reception. A band played soft rock music as the guests danced on the wooden floor constructed for the occasion. Almost a year ago, when she'd arrived in Capri, a woman determined to have a new life, she could not have imagined the riches in love and happiness that awaited her.

"I think everyone's having too good a time to leave," she said. "Or to miss us." Among the guests, she could see her parents laughing together. Her mother glowed with an inner happiness Cat had rarely seen. Soon after Tinsley's wedding, Cat's father had stopped drinking. He'd also started divorce proceedings against Nolan and began courting Cat's mother. Her mom hadn't welcomed him with open arms, but he'd worked hard to convince her he still loved her. Staring down at her parents, elation, sweet as wedding cake, coursed through Cat.

The staff and owners from Vault occupied two large tables where they laughed and talked together. Alex had flown them all in from San Francisco. Bobbie St. James catered their wedding as his gift. Because the restaurant had to close for five days, Alex had paid the owners what they would have earned had the restaurant been open. Her new husband was as generous as he was loving.

"Let our guests party." Alex kissed her gently. "They won't miss us. We will make love now."

She wound her arms around his neck. "Sounds good to me."

With a soft chuckle, he picked her up and carried her through the open doors to their bedroom. With tenderness, he laid her on the bed and sank down next to her. "I love you, my Cat."

"I will love you always, Alex."

While the band played a romantic song, Cat and Alex went to the stars and back together the first time as husband and wife, promising many more magical Capri nights.

ALL ABOUT CARA MARSI

An award-winning and eclectic author, Cara Marsi is published in romantic suspense, paranormal romance, and contemporary romance. She loves a good love story, and believes that everyone deserves a second chance at love. Sexy, sweet, thrilling, or magical, Cara's stories are first and foremost about the love.

Read about all Cara's books and sign up for her newsletter at www.caramarsi.com. She's on Facebook, Twitter, Goodreads, and Pinterest and is always interested in making new friends.

Author's Note: Thank you for reading my story. I hope you enjoyed this romantic trip to the Isle of Capri. I've visited Capri twice, and it is indeed bewitching.

Books by Cara Marsi

A Catered Romance
A Cat's Tale & Other Love Stories
(All stories in this anthology are available separately)
A Cinderella Christmas
A Groom for Christmas
Accidental Love
Capri Nights
Cursed Mates
Her Forever Husband
Her Snow White Christmas (Snow Globe Magic Book 1)
Her Frog Prince Holiday (Snow Globe Magic Book 2)
Logan's Redemption (Redemption Book 1)
Franco's Fortune (Redemption Book 2)
Luke's Temptation (Redemption Book 3)
Love Potion
Loving Or Nothing
Murder, Mi Amore
Season of Magic Holiday Boxed Set
Season of Surprises Holiday Boxed Set
Storm of Desire
Sweet Temptations
Sweet Temptations Boxed Set
The Marriage Coin Boxed Set
The One Who Got Away
The Ring
Wedding Dreams Boxed Set

Coming Early 2016, Her Red Riding Hood Valentine
(Snow Globe Magic Book 3)

Read excerpts at www.caramarsi.com

All books available at online booksellers

A Catered Romance, A Groom for Christmas, Capri Nights, Cursed Mates, Franco's Fortune, Logan's Redemption, Loving Or Nothing, Luke's Temptation, Murder, Mi Amore, Season of Magic, and The Marriage Coin are also available in print.

Potato & Onion Frittata
(Much like the spinach, mushroom, potato frittata
Cat and Alex share)

- 1 large red onion
- 1 Tbsp. olive oil
- 2 medium red potatoes (about 12 oz.), cut into ½ inch pieces
- Salt and pepper
- ¼ cup fresh flat-leaf parsley, chopped
- 8 large eggs
- 1 cup whole milk
- 4 oz. extra-sharp Cheddar

Heat oven to 400 degrees F. Finely chop the onion.

Heat oil in a large oven-safe nonstick skillet over medium heat. Add the potatoes and chopped onion, season with salt and pepper to taste, and cook, covered, stirring occasionally, for 7 minutes. Uncover and continue cooking, stirring occasionally, until the potatoes are golden brown and just tender, 12 to 15 minutes more. If desired, when the potatoes are almost done, stir in fresh spinach and sliced mushrooms and saute. Stir in the parsley.

While the potatoes and onions are cooking, in a medium bowl, whisk together the eggs, milk, and ¼ Tsp. each salt and pepper; stir in the cheese.

Pour the egg mixture into the skillet and stir to distribute the ingredients. Transfer the skillet to the oven and bake until the frittata is puffed, brown around the edges, and a knife inserted into the center comes out clean, 14 to 16 minutes.

Serve with a salad and crusty bread.